About the author

Jonathan H. Kita (Jon) was born in Southington, Connecticut, in 1957. He grew up in New England before moving to North Carolina, where he earned a Bachelor of Science degree from North Carolina State University. Jon currently resides in Chesapeake, Virginia.

THE NEWTON PROJECT

Jon Kita

THE NEWTON PROJECT

Vanguard Press

VANGUARD PAPERBACK

© Copyright 2022
Jon Kita

The right of Jon Kita to be identified as author of
this work has been asserted by him in accordance with the
Copyright, Designs and Patents Act 1988.

All Rights Reserved

No reproduction, copy or transmission of this publication
may be made without written permission.
No paragraph of this publication may be reproduced,
copied or transmitted save with the written permission of the
publisher, or in accordance with the provisions
of the Copyright Act 1956 (as amended).

Any person who commits any unauthorised act in relation to
this publication may be liable to criminal
prosecution and civil claims for damages.

A CIP catalogue record for this title is
available from the British Library.

ISBN 978-1-80016-194-8

*Vanguard Press is an imprint of
Pegasus Elliot MacKenzie Publishers Ltd.*
www.pegasuspublishers.com

First Published in 2022

**Vanguard Press
Sheraton House Castle Park
Cambridge England**

Printed & Bound in Great Britain

Dedication

This book is dedicated to scientists and science fiction readers whose paths often cross over time.

This is a work of fiction. Names, characters, businesses, places, events and incidents are either the products of the author's imagination or used in a fictitious manner. Any resemblance to actual persons, living or dead, or actual events is purely coincidental.

US Air Force Indo-Pacific Command

The B-52 Stratofortress lifted from its base in Guam breaking through the low-level clouds… unannounced. The pilot in command today, Capt. "Bones" Beckman, banked the aircraft to a westerly heading as the co-pilot rechecked the mission data in the computer.

In addition to the pilot and co-pilot, four other crew members were aboard for today's mission—electronic weapons officer, navigator, radar navigator, and surveillance officer, a position recently added in the huge aft area of the bomber which they called the pit.

This heavy bomber was on another important mission. Today, however, the bomber carried no bombs, no cruise missiles, and no gunner capability.

The Stratofortress is a heavy bomber with a résumé that few aircraft could ever match and over sixty years of service defending the United States in many theatres around the globe. No longer the nuclear payload prowler of the Russian Bear, the aircraft was now under the Global Strike Command as part of a continuous presence with the much newer B-1 and B-2 aircraft.

What had not changed was the basic design of the B-52, a solid platform with swept wings, large payload capacity, and most importantly, negligible metal fatigue after many years of service. It was well-engineered by

Boeing. The eight original engines, Pratt & Whitney low-bypass turbofan J-57s, gave the Stratofortress a typical range of over 8,800 miles and easy refueling when needed for around-the-clock mission capabilities. This aircraft boasted enhanced P&W TF33 engines, giving the aircraft better thrust-to-weight ratio and ever-improving flight range and altitude.

B-52s have been upgraded and heavily modified over the years as new Joint Direct Attack Munitions, air-to-surface missiles, nuclear tipped cruise missiles and other munitions became available, largely unknown when the aircraft was built.

Capt. Beckman's bomber was equipped with FLIR forward-looking infrared optical sensors, as well as older but exceptionally reliable imaging and recording devices going back to earlier applications from the SR-71 Blackbird supersonic spy plane era. This Stratofortress was boldly equipped as a big, yet subsonic, surveillance aircraft.

Capt. Beckman's mission was under control of the US Indo-Pacific Command, a joint exercise with Japan's air self-defense force.

The plane picked up speed and altitude, and Capt. Beckman came over the intercom. "Greetings, crew, can I get a comm check from each of you?"

In turn, each member responded with "check" and a few "good mornings."

"Thank you. You were purposely *not briefed* before we left base. This big, old bird is equipped for a new mission. Our mission today is 'Cobra-1'. You can see we have no bombs aboard, only recently installed optics and surveillance equipment. We are heading toward the South China Sea to hopefully gain insight on the Chinese Army airforce island bases currently in development. Our orders are basic intel: take some images and scans to see what level of readiness these new air bases constitute, flex some American muscle, and keep the skies clear for continuous training missions."

The navigator, Lt. Col. Hall, piped in. "Captain, certainly we have high altitude aircraft that can do this work. Why send in a Strato?"

"Copy that," replied Capt. Beckman. "It appears Washington wants us to assert out rights to airspace over the South China Sea and the waters below. Washington reiterating that this is internationally recognized air space, and we do not expect any company up here."

Lt. Col. Stevens, electronics weapons officer, came on the comm. "Sir, this is easy satellite mapping. I'm with Hall. This BUFF we are flying, or as some refer to us, Big Ugly Fat Fellow, is a surveillance plane. Will fighter escorts be joining us, sir?"

Capt. Beckman responded to the whole team. "I appreciate your interest and enthusiasm for this mission, but since Washington does not give me satellite orbit mapping information for our Strategic Defense Initiative, we will follow our orders with a high level of execution. Going forward, we can expect more frequent missions like today—more training flights over international waters. No fighter escorts in today's playbook because we might appear as a first strike mission on radar. We do not want the Chinese all worked up. I have got to tell you that I think today's mission will likely become more frequent so let's all get to work. We should be over the South China Sea, less than 2,000 miles due west, in just a few hours.

"What's the weather looking like?" asked Capt. Beckman.

"It looks clear with light clouds, fifty-mile visibility," replied Radar Navigator Sanchez. Should be smooth weather with a slight chop moving through 10,000."

"Thanks," replied Beckman.

The plane continued to climb and the captain mentally reviewed his situation… instruments good, engines RPM's green, rate of climb right on target.

As the aircraft leveled off at 40,000 feet, Co-pilot Hall eased back again on the throttles.

The crew settled into their assignments.

Capt. Beckman came over the system again, "Sanchez, you got your lights on?"

"Yes, sir," replied Sanchez. "FLIR radar is active and the rear targeting pods are covering our six, Captain. No aircraft detected at this time."

"Mr. James, any surface contacts?"

"Negative, no surface contacts, sir."

"Copy," replied the captain.

About time for a coffee lift Beckman thought to himself as he reached for his thermos.

EWO Stevens came over the comm. "Sir, a couple of us are new to the team here. We were wondering how you got the name 'Bones', if you don't mind, sir."

The captain took a sip of his coffee, smiled, and looked over at Co-pilot Hall, a fine-looking gym-hardened African American Air Force officer.

Co-pilot Hall smiled back at Bones and said, "Well, it's a fair question, Captain. Do you want to tell them or should I?"

Bones picked up his mic and said, "Okay, fair question, I guess. We'll tell you a little history."

"My grandfather was a B17 pilot during World War II. He was stationed in Deenthorpe, England, and eventually did bombing missions all the way to Berlin. German Messerschmitt 109s, later jet-powered 262s, were giving bombers a high mortality rate—sometimes fifty percent bomber losses on single missions. Co-pilot Hall, please continue," Bones said into the comm.

"So," replied Hall, "turns out *my* granddad was also a pilot during WWII. He also flew planes all the way into Berlin. Grandpappy Hall applied for 8th Air Force but was denied, but he did not quit. He applied again and was accepted for P-51 fighter training and later assigned to the Red Tails."

"Are you kidding me?" replied EWO Stevens. "I knew you guys were military brats but I had no idea."

The whole crew was now listening intently.

"Tuskegee Airmen, right?" Sanchez knew that must be correct.

"Damn right, Sanchez," replied Bones. "So, my grandfather used that name because the only thing he figured the military would send home to his wife was whatever bones were left when they were shot down."

"I know," commented Radar Navigator James, "of how the Red Tails would protect the B-17 Flying Fortresses all the way to Berlin and back, and the Redtail's never lost a bomber!"

"Damn right!" replied Co-pilot Hall, and they all laughed together.

The crew settled back as they moved closer to the target area.

Most of the crew had little sleep while their thoughts raced about their unknown mission.

Bones Beckman had little sleep because he *did* know the mission. He knew there was no routine recon flight near Chinese installations, but he did not want to alarm the crew.

South China Sea

The Chengdu J-20 Dragon stealth fighter flew with purpose and agility while making a hard subsonic turn over the Spratly Islands above the South China Sea. The pilot engaged the air brakes briefly. The large red star on the side of the aircraft, surrounded by four smaller stars shone brightly over the newly constructed airfield below. The airbase was built as an artificial island specifically for the new Chinese aircraft. The weather was clear and warm. Pilot Yang Wei of the People's Liberation Army Air Force (PLAAF) had been testing these aircraft for several years. He knew their Dragon would be formidable not only against a Mig-29 but also very capable against the American fighters if necessary.

Col. Wei detested the US geopolitical dominance and considered them aggressors and provocateurs against his country. *American naval vessels be damned*, he thought to himself. He was happy that President Li was militarizing many areas of the South China Sea. Col. Wei smiled ever so slightly, knowing the Dragon Fighter was finally in production. This version had a larger fuel tank than the earlier J-10s, giving him a combat radius over 1200 kilometers. Aerodynamic features designed for stealth and radar-absorbing coatings made the aircraft highly undetectable. Best of all the advancements were immensely powerful WS-15 engines able to super cruise without the use of afterburners. He landed the aircraft on freshly made tarmac and taxied his way to another J-20. These were the first Chinese fighters to land on the new base.

Beijing

The newly elected President Li addressed assembled members of the National Committee in Beijing. "Our government has claimed a large area of the South China Sea as our sovereign territory officially since 1947, including maritime rights. I want to emphasize this even further by saying this territory has belonged to China for centuries!"

Col. Wei was watching the address with rapt attention, and he knew this was also a subtle mocking to the US who claimed international rights to many areas.

"Vietnam was a poor, undeveloped, neighboring country," said President Li. "However, the US could not overcome Vietnam with all their strength and weapons! Vietnam would not give in and did not fear the giant! The islands in the South China Sea belong to us, and we are expanding our air forces there at this time," President Li declared defiantly. "We claim other territories nearby as well as the Spratly Islands." President Li continued, calling the US "a giant still oppressing the Japanese some seventy years after the war." He was becoming more passionate. "It was the United States who dropped nuclear bombs on Japan in 1945, and who today station a nuclear aircraft carrier there while Americans happily buy Japanese products by the thousands!"

"The people in Washington are trying to colonize global business, undermining our economy with poorly conceived tariffs. They are telling us to stay out of Taiwan. They falsely accuse us of stealing their technology. They are stopping and boarding our merchant vessels without authority. The South China Sea is our territory and any foreign military violating our sovereignty will be handled with quick resolve! We will not tolerate this any longer!"

There was a thunderous ovation in quick response to this bold statement by President Li.

***

Capt. Beckman loved the serenity of the early morning. Somehow, it reminded him of how truly important his service to his country was. He must always be on guard to protect that serenity for his homeland, and he understood only too well just how fragile serenity is. Peace is easily shattered. Hostilities are always slow to end. This morning, Capt. Beckman looked at the horizon and saw nothing but clear sky. "Mr. Hall, you got the aircraft while I hit the head?"

"Sure, Captain," replied the co-pilot.

"I may be a few minutes. I want to speak with Major Campbell back in the pit."

Hall responded, "I understand they added a surveillance officer to the mission."

"That's affirmative," said the captain.

"Captain, I did not know B52s had something called the pit, sir."

"Have you taken a close look at the electronics back there? The story I heard was a couple guys from Raytheon were running tests. The consoles were so high around the surveillance seat they looked down one day and said the seat was in a pit."

"So the name kind of stuck."

Bones made his way toward the back of the aircraft.

"How do we look, Mr. Campbell?" asked the captain.

"We enter the South China Sea airspace shortly. As you know, my job is to optically record this area closely and carefully. Bravo Command needs accurate intel on these Chinese bases, or we will be coming back for another run over the same real estate.

"Can you go to heading 2-7-5 when I give you the affirmative shortly? That will put us just south of Spratly Islands air defense and well outside the twelve-mile Chinese Air Defense Zone."

"Copy that," replied Capt. Beckman.

They continued their heading with only intermittent bumps—pretty smooth air for the heavy bomber.

"Captain, requesting 2-7-5," said Campbell.

"Acknowledged." The aircraft began a gentle banking slightly more northward.

"Sir, 2-7-5 brings us slightly closer over the base, and we don't know what air defenses we are up against." Co-pilot Hall was a bit anxious. "We might stir up a nest of hornets if the base is active."

"Well," replied Beckman, "that's exactly what we are here to find out. Satellite images are not precise, but we know the base construction is moving quickly. We need a closer look to see how close to operational they are."

"The optics are active and surveillance recordings are live," said Officer Campbell. "Just keep us going nice and steady."

Co-pilot Hall checked the artificial horizon. "Holding steady 2-7-5, Captain. Engine pod three had spiked RPMs but are back to normal. Frankly, I am not used to flying this B-52 without a heavy payload. The trim characteristics seem more responsive."

"Yeah, that's normal," replied the captain with a slight grin. "Most missions, we return with the same payload we started with. I guess that's a good thing. In the old days, we'd leave with four nuclear bombs and return with four bombs."

"Just hold her steady so Campbell can get his image data."

"Just a little while longer, and we can think about our return trip back to the barn," the captain said quietly to Co-pilot Hall.

An unexpected alarm sounded.

"Captain, we are being tracked and scanned." Sanchez spoke with an anxious edge in his voice.

"Say again?" asked the captain.

Sanchez was trying to maintain a calm composure, but concern was evident in his raised voice, as he reiterated, "We have been picked up on Chinese radar."

Beckman could hear a steady beeping from the FLIR.

"Do you want to change course?" asked Co-pilot Hall.

"Stay 2-7-5," replied Capt. Beckman, as his concern grew. "Make new altitude at 35 thousand."

"Any surface contacts?"

"Negative, no surface contacts," replied Sanchez, as he silenced the ear-piercing alarms.

The captain addressed the crew. "We are over international waters. Remain on course. Stay on alert."

Surveillance Officer Campbell added, "Sir, it appears that Spratly Island has an operational radar system. Their mainland base would not be able to pick up this far out."

"Affirmative, add that to the mission notes, Mr. Sanchez."

"Any aircraft contacts?"

"Negative, sir."

With the alarm off, the plane remained quiet as the crew verified instruments. The constant humming of the 8 engines and occasional bump went unnoticed as they were focused on their work.

Co-Pilot Hall verified coordinates and spoke to the captain. "Are we cutting into the air defense too close?"

"Like I said earlier, I'm not coming back to map this a second time."

"Copy that," said Co-Pilot Hall.

Department of Defense
Washington, DC

The president met with the Joint Chiefs and was not happy with the extreme and controversial words of President Li. He asked his analyst, Chen Yang, and Ambassador to China, Jon Wiggins, for an overview and analytical comments.

Chen Yang commented quickly. "For many years, the Chinese wanted only growth through working people—let the people do without struggle. They worked for prosperity, but over time gained only complacency and poverty. Over a century ago, Chinese workers came to America to build railroads, to do work too hard for many others, and find jobs, not unlike myself today. However, many were treated less than equal by some people of prominence, who sought to cash in on the low-wage labor. Chinese were designated as uneducated peasants destined for hard labor only. What you are seeing from President Li is years of Chinese progression both economically, politically, and now militarily. He believes in 'ai chi,' let the enemy defeat themselves. Or to put it another way, do not attack a superior enemy head-on. Weaken him from the sides, then kill the enemy when he is weak. A wolf cannot kill a bear. A wolf pack can kill the biggest bear."

"Ambassador Wiggins, can you add something to this discussion?" asked the president unassumingly.

"Sir, Analyst Chen Yang has given you some insight as to what is happening in China today. I can only remind you that China is an important trading partner. Almost fifty percent of goods from China go through the South China Sea, and we see this area being militarized. Economic ramifications are significant. China's sea power is formidable and their air force, the PLAAF, is on track with full production of their J-20 Strike Fighter. Furthermore, the Chinese government has just ruled to discard long-held term limits for the office of president. In other words, President Li will be president of China for many years to come. He is young, aggressive, and determined to build a strong military. He does not follow the way of his predecessors, as Chen Yang has just said. He is the new wolf in the committee... not easily persuaded. In short, sir, the Asia geopolitical map is reminding me of Europe around 1940. This China is willing to defend its territorial sovereignty at any cost, including a pre-emptive attack on foreign navy vessels in the South China Seas which we ascertain to include American. We are providing surveillance aircraft to confirm a Chinese airbase may soon be operational in the Spratly Islands. It is a sophisticated artificial island specifically designed for their airbase and missile installations. A second artificial island base is also under construction at the

Paracel Islands. We are doing re-con work to find their level of readiness."

"Admiral Jackson, in your estimation, what is our next step?" asked the president inquisitively.

"We can deploy CVN-5 Strike Group from Yokosuka in forty-eight hours with eight-ship support and one fast-attack sub. We need to stop the Chinese provocations and control shipping lanes. President Li will not attempt a conflict and must ask for a diplomatic solution with you, Mr. President. It is his only good option, sir. President Kobe of Japan supports this and says time is short."

***

Cobra-1

"Captain, we have a bogey on our six!" exclaimed Surveillance Officer Campbell, with alarm in his voice. "Correction, we have two! Two bogeys closing fast, sir!"

"What are they?" asked the captain.

"I can confirm shortly, sir, but by their exceptionally low radar signature it could be a couple of Dragons, their front-line fighters."

Bones looked over at Hall and said, "I have the stick. Call this into Base Command now, Mr. Hall."

"Affirmative, Captain," replied Co-pilot Hall.

"Bravo Charlie, Bravo Charlie, we have encountered enemy fighters. Can you verify our position? Copy."

Campbell came back over the comm. "Captain, one fighter directly off our six, and the second is coming up along our port side, sir".

The captain heard more alarms sounding from both the Electronic Warfare Station and Campbell's surveillance equipment.

"Bravo Command is acknowledging your transmission," replied a base command officer back in Guam. We are escalating your situation. Keep us apprised."

"Affirmative."

The Chinese fighter was only fifty feet away from the B-52 and easing up the left side where the captain's seat was situated.

As the fighter pulled up even with the captain's window, the Chinese pilot gave a short burst of front nose 50 mm cannon fire. He quickly got Capt. Beckman's attention. *Serenity is so easily shattered.*

Beckman looked over at the fighter and immediately confirmed it was a front-line Dragon. The Chinese red star was just below the pilot's canopy. The captain also noted the wing-mounted air-to-air missiles, and knew the other Dragon that was on his six was locked and loaded.

Bones looked at Hall and said, "This bogey just fired his nose cannon, and the second fighter is holding position directly behind us. Please inform Bravo Charlie."

The Chinese pilot pointed at the right side of his helmet in a motion to Pilot Beckman. He fired his nose cannon again.

Beckman pulled his microphone and set it to international frequency.

"Do you copy?" said Beckman into the microphone.

The Chinese pilot responded slowly in somewhat broken English. "You are over Chinese restricted air space with a first strike nuclear weapons offensive aircraft."

Capt. Beckman replied, "We are over international waters with no weapons on this aircraft. This is a training flight."

Co-pilot Hall looked over at Bones and said, "Base Command has confirmed our location outside the Chinese proximity zone. Stay on mission objectives and keep BC informed of Chinese hostilities."

Backman looked over at the Chinese pilot and motioned to the left side of his helmet that he was going to respond.

"We are over international waters and international air space. This is an American military aircraft on a training mission," replied Beckman.

There was a delayed response, and Beckman suspected the Chinese pilot was receiving instructions from his superiors.

"I am Capt. Chen of the Chinese Army Air Force. You have initiated an act of war. We will escort you to an adequate landing strip on the mainland to confirm your aircraft has no offensive weapons. Please go to heading 280 now."

Bones looked over at Hall. Always calm and clear-headed, both men had a singular focus on the situation at hand as their minds automatically analyzed and strategized. Yet both were astounded.

"Call this into BC, Officer Hall. Looks like the Chinese want a confrontation up here."

"Let them know the Chinese pilots are becoming more aggressive."

Capt. Beckman held his heading at 2-7-5. He was anxious to start his return leg back to Guam as soon as mapping was done or as soon as Base Command gave them new orders to potentially abort.

The Chinese pilot spoke again. "Turn your aircraft to 2-8-0 or we will be forced to destroy your aircraft!"

The captain looked over to the Chinese pilot in disbelief. Capt. Chen made a hand motion for the B-52 to change direction.

Beckman looked over at Hall and said, "The Chinese are trying to start a war." He picked up the mic and asked the Chinese pilot to repeat the communication.

"I agree." Bones concurred with Hall. "A big damn war if they don't stand down."

"Bravo Charlie, this is Cobra-1. The Chinese pilot is ordering us to land, or they will destroy this aircraft. Do you copy?"

He paused for a reply. Hall glanced at Bones. "It appears we have few options. We can try to bank to port, further away from Chinese territory, hoping they do not fire. Or, we can eject and take our chances, and they will not get the aircraft. Or, we can land this plane, be arrested as spies, and be put in a communist prison for an indefinite time. Possibly forever."

Beckman replied again to Bravo Charlie. "Base Command, we got any friendlies in the area?"

"Negative," replied Base Command. "We are checking Marine Base Okinawa but there are no marine aircraft that have the fuel or distance to assist you."

A new name came over the comm. "Cobra-1, Cobra-1, do you read me? Over."

"Who the hell is that?" Bones asked Major Campbell in the surveillance pit.

"Sir, it's a marine pilot."

"This is Cobra-1," replied Bones.

"Copy that, sir. I am Major Gabe Gossich on a re-certification training run west of the Philippines. I got your transmissions on the back-channel and I understand you have some Chinese bogeys. Am I correct, sir?"

"Worse than you can imagine, Major. We have two Chinese fighters telling us to land or be shot down. Copy."

The Chinese pilot motioned to Capt. Beckman more urgently.

"Yes, I copy," replied the marine pilot.

Bones continued, "Major Gossich, there are no other friendlies in our area, you are too far east to provide support, but we appreciate the communication, sir."

Hall asked Bones, "What are you going to reply to the Chinese pilot?"

Beckman did not reply to Co-pilot Hall. Without hesitation, he switched frequency and spoke into the mic to the Chinese pilot. "Staying on course 2-7-5, we have confirmed we are flying international airspace." He looked left toward the Chinese fighter pilot.

Major Gossich continued flying west toward the B-52. He lit the afterburner and climbed into increasingly thin, fast air. He set his altimeter to 50,000 feet, near ceiling maximum, and leveled off. He throttled the aircraft back to conserve fuel and began calculating fuel consumption versus speed. He quickly came to some realizations. He knew time was critical for Cobra-1. He knew equally as well he did not have enough fuel to intercept.

The B-52 was also flying away from him. He did not have the fuel for even a one-way mission. But Gossich calculated he could still head west and recalculate fuel. He followed his instincts.

Co-pilot Hall continued to copy Bravo Charlie. The situation was grim. The enemy pilot persistently provocative. They were running out of time.

The message from Base Command was "abort mission."

Beckman began a slow bank to port, trying to head away.

The Chinese pilot gave a harsh command. "American pilot, you are to turn to heading 3-5-0 north or be destroyed!"

Capt. Beckman informed the crew they may have to eject. If so, they would try to stay together.

In a B-52, the pilot, co-pilot, gunner and EW officer seats eject upwards. The remaining seats eject downward. The opposing trajectories would naturally separate them.

The Chinese fighter fired his nose cannon one more time.

He repeated, "This is final communication. Head 3-5-0 or we will fire."

Beckman looked at Hall. "If we are going to eject, I want us at 10,000 feet or lower. I am going to turn to heading 3-5-0 north and start descending to buy us some time."

The aircraft began to bank right and to the north. Both enemy fighters followed closely, one bogey directly behind the B-52 and the second off the port wing.

Carrier Strike Group 5 (CSG-5) was put on alert. Based in Yokosuka, Japan, the group included a Nimitz-class aircraft carrier, three Ticonderoga-class cruisers, five Arleigh Burke-class destroyers, and the fast-attack sub, *Washington.*

They were to prepare to deploy, if needed, to the ever more dangerous waters of the South China Seas.

The B-52 was on heading 3-5-0 and began a slow descent.

Bones said to Hall, "We have to slow down and get lower before we can even think about ejecting."

Hall replied, "Copy. Do you think these Chinese pilots know they are about to start a serious conflict?"

"They have probably been told these are Chinese-protected waters to try a stunt like this." Hall didn't think Chinese pilots would go rogue.

"Maybe that's just what they want, a conflict." Bones was sick at the thought. Despite his confidence in the American military, Bones knew well that such a conflict would be costly in many ways.

"Sir, we will not have much more time over internationally recognized waters. Then it's maybe an hour to the Chinese mainland and the landing site."

"If we have to eject, I don't want to be close to the mainland. I want this bird spread out across the ocean floor as far as possible."

Suddenly Surveillance Officer Campbell came over the comm. "Bogey bearing 0-9-0. Air contact is on an intercept course, sir!"

"Captain, it has a marine call sign. It's one of ours, sir."

"Cobra-1, Cobra-1, this is Major Gossich. Do you read me? Over."

"Yes, Major, we read you."

"I am east at 50,000 and low on fuel. I figured I might have a chance of interception if you changed your course from westerly, which you did to the north. I have followed your transmissions to Bravo Charlie."

"Affirmative," replied Bones. "One on our six, and the second is still off the port wing.

"Captain, if I am able to fire before I run out of fuel, I will need you to kill all your engines. Otherwise, my air-to-air missiles will lock onto your greater engine heat signature—not the fighter!"

"What's your ETA, Major?"

"I should be in range in about five minutes."

"Affirmative."

Major Campbell came back on the comm. "Captain, Major Gossich is flying an F-35 Lightning II Stealth, according to his radar call sign. What I am saying, Captain, is his fighter has Electro-Optical Targeting System, what we call EOTS, and the Chinese won't see him coming. Maybe our odds just picked up, sir."

Bones throttled back more, and the B-52 began to descend.

The Chinese pilot spoke, "Maintain your heading and altitude. Do not descend until instructed."

"Goose to Cobra-1, two minutes until intercept. Be ready to kill all engines! I won't get a second chance."

"I'm losing engine power." Bones spoke back to the Chinese pilot, trying to create a moment of confusion."

"Okay, kill engines!" replied Major Gossich.

The second Chinese pilot asked for permission to fire from Capt. Chen.

"Do not fire," replied Capt. Chen. "They are crashing their plane, a good ending."

The F-35 Lightning II began a fast, hot descent! Air-to-air missiles locked! Distance confirmed. Gossich pulled the trigger and saw the missile trail away in an instant.

"Bones, missile fired," replied the major.

Seconds later, the Chinese Dragon directly behind the B-52 exploded!

Capt. Chen, off the port side of the aircraft saw the explosion and broke left.

Major Gossich hit his air brakes and trailed the second Dragon in a tight roll, and opened up with both side-mounted cannons. The Dragon could not escape! Flames billowed as the Chinese fighter headed down toward the ocean and disintegrated.

Bones and Hall worked feverishly to restart the B-52 engines. They were descending fast!

"Altitude 5,000 feet and falling!" Hall called out to Bones.

Gossich pulled out of his roll, and with whatever fuel remained, pulled along the portside of the B-52 as they both leveled off just above the water.

"What a sight, I can see the white caps on the water!" said Hall.

"Yeah, and there's Major Gossich off to port!"

"I got engine flame out here, Bones. Call me in."

"Already done that, Major. Can't thank you enough. Great shooting!"

Goose pulled his ejection seat as Bones followed him with his eyes until the parachute opened. The white parachute slowly descended into blue desolation. They all knew there were no friendly ships nearby. A sight Bones would never forget!

Newton, the Person and His Science

It's a bright, sunny Christmas Day in 1642. Amid the joyous Glorias sung out to celebrate the birth of the Christ child, another baby boy is born. Though not a savior for mankind, Sir Isaac Newton is not an ordinary English lad. He will prove to be one of the greatest scientific minds, unlocking secrets of the universe and vastly expanding our knowledge of the planet Earth. As a youngster, he attended school in Grantham at The King's School and later attended Trinity College in Cambridge. While studying at Cambridge, he gained knowledge of the scientific minds and teachings of Aristotle, Descartes, and Galileo, and his sharp mind expanded in both knowledge and wonder. As Newton matured from a child to a man, his inquisitive mind searched for answers beyond the scope of what books could give him, and from the relative comfort of home, Newton continued his studies and developed his theory of gravity as well as his universal law of gravitation equation. He described the relationships between force, matter, and acceleration. All and all, Newton paved the way for a myriad of inventions used today, including many applications we use unknowingly.

For example, when a professional quarterback throws a ball toward his receiver, he is calculating many sciences at once—the spiral spin on the ball to reduce drag, the acceleration in which he throws the football, the angle of the football when it is thrown, and the movement of his receiver at the anticipated point of the catch. The quarterback may not be thinking at all how gravity plays its role in the way the football moves away from the Earth's pull and makes its way back down again.

Sir Isaac Newton's Law of Universal Gravitation regarding gravitational theory is his most famous discovery. As laid out in this theory, all particles in the universe exert gravitational force. Physicists following him through the years move slightly closer to revealing more secrets of subatomic particles—the fundamental theory to explain the reason for our universe. In his Law of Inertia, Newton explains his idea of the three laws of motion—objects remain either at rest or in motion unless acted upon. They move with the same velocity and in a straight line.

Suppose a man is weightless in a spaceship while in orbit around the Earth. Now imagine a rocket fires this weightless man off into space. As he accelerates, this man's weight (mass) feels heavier. Now stretch your imagination more and imagine we could magically move this man in his capsule on the moon. He now feels about a sixth of his weight versus his normal gravity on Earth. A two-hundred-pound man would weigh about thirty-three pounds on the moon. The gravitational force he feels while stationary is the same type of force he feels while accelerating in space. This spaceman has now experienced gravitational acceleration as well as gravity due to his mass. The bigger the mass, the smaller the acceleration. Without gravity, the universe would potentially exist as a floating cloud.

Newton discovered how key gravity is to our existence. The force keeping planets, stars, and the universe in order. Gravity attracts. We know of no negative naturally occurring mass. Likewise, there is no negative gravity. This simple, yet overwhelming impactful concept is key to how the universe works. This is the invisible force holding us all here and prevents us from floating off into space. The mass of the Earth holds us in place. Gravity is a relatively weak force, but nonetheless, it is the precise force required to make the universe and planets possible. If gravity had a greater pull, the universe would likely be made of black holes—huge masses with extremely powerful gravitational pull. If gravitational pull were too weak, the universe would be a ball of dust and floating particles. As a precise and perfect balance, gravity counters the planets' orbits. Some scientists agree if they were to try creating a gravity by mathematical computation, their equation results could be like carrying the equation to one hundred digits, and all would have to be perfect! One digit mathematically wrong, and gravity would not work—could not work—

and could not keep universes and galaxies in balance. God's design was flawless!

Einstein's Theory of Relativity looks at gravity in a different kind of way. Einstein describes gravity as bending or distorting space around mass and energy, rather than looking to explain the reason for the existence of gravity. This perspective of gravity as a curvature of the four-dimensional space-time continuum brings understanding to how light can bend around objects, such as a ball under a blanket causing a curvature in an otherwise flat plane. Gravitational waves move through space as ripples created by accelerating masses. In all the universes, this magic we call gravity is a relatively weak force, yet its attraction and cumulative effect are massive and unstoppable.

***

Beijing, China

PLA, (Peoples Liberation Army) is the armed forces of the People's Republic of China. This is not only the ruling communist political party, it is the five professional service branches including Army, Navy, Air Force, Rocket Force, and Strategic Support Forces. It is arguably one of the three largest military operations in the world and has the second-largest defense budget in the world behind the US. It falls under the command of the CMC, Central Military Commission. The chairman of the CMC had a plan for many years but only recently was it approved by its new President Li: stop American imperialism by sinking one of its nuclear carriers, thereby making American strike forces obsolete in the Asian Pacific and questionable around the world. Chinese military forces would now be more equal. The plan was simple; the execution complex. The plan: Engage an American aircraft or surface vessel into a conflict in order to bring a modern nuclear carrier into Chinese waters. Identify the target and counter American radar and surveillance systems. Surprise launch of massive DB-21 missiles using satellite targeting of the carrier. Follow the DB-21 strike quickly and unexpectedly with stealth fighters equipped with newly developed *Qiangda* cruise missiles in overwhelming numbers.

***

When word reached the Chinese air commander that two of his new aircraft had been destroyed, he was outraged. A communication was sent to President Li, and all branches of the PLAAC went on alert.

The Chinese Air Force quickly began to send more fighters from the mainland to Spratly Island to reinforce its newest air base.

The Chinese air base commander sent a message to President Li. "This time an American military aircraft got away, but it will not happen again."

Perhaps, thought President Li, *perhaps this is just the opportunity we need.*

Carrier Strike Group 5 (CSG-5) formed off Yokosuka with three Ticonderoga-class cruisers and five Arleigh Burke-class destroyers. Fast-attack sub, *Washington* would join them as they entered the dangerous waters of the South China Sea. The *Washington* was a forward-deployed Virginia-class submarine that had been conducting surveillance of the Chinese naval activities. The *Washington* had received orders to search for a downed marine pilot. The air base development on the Spratly Islands had been monitored by both satellite and the *Washington's* optical radar systems over several months. ComStar5 was the US satellite positioned closely over the South China Sea and part of the strike force defense system's Cooperative Engagement Capability. This provided a real-time mix of satellite, air and surface capabilities with integration for far better defense against a multiple-enemy offensive strike. Satellites in higher orbit can cover greater areas but with less quality imaging. Lower orbit satellites are clearer, but more would be needed to cover this area in the future. Most satellite imaging was still being prioritized for the Middle East, North Korea, and Russian priorities.

A Chinese weather satellite had been in orbit 200 kilometers from ComStar5 for several years, and as far as the military could determine, it was just that, a weather satellite. It was, in fact, a Trojan horse.

While a US carrier is a big four-acre floating airfield at over 100,000 tons, the sea is an exponentially more enormous area, and the carrier is always moving, not needing time to stop and refuel. Tracking one is an arduous task—by even a very modern and well-equipped country. Submarines are a lurking threat, but the underwater detection capabilities by both the cruisers and destroyers provide a nearly impenetrable defense against even Russia's newest nuclear submarines. Chinese submarines are not nearly as stealthy and are more easily detected. Mines are a potential threat to any surface vessel, but many mines would be required for a strategic defense. The Chinese shipping lanes were heavily used by Chinese commercial shipping. Mines cannot differentiate friend from foe. The *Washington* detected no mines on its patrol. The greatest threat to the American strike force was short-range ICBMs—specifically Chinese DB-21s and 26s, as well as fighter-launched missiles.

With a moving carrier, ICBMs are difficult to target on surface vessels. Many would be needed as a carrier with twenty-minute radar notice is miles away from the initial target area. A carrier is 500 miles away or more in a twenty-four-hour period.

As the strike force entered the South China Sea, the aircraft carrier *Independence* launched its first E-2C Hawkeye. A Grumman RQ-4 Global Hawk equipped with JSTAR, (Joint Surveillance Targeting and Attack Radar System) had been deployed twenty-four hours earlier and was still on patrol for the strike force. Had the Global Hawk detected a threat the carrier could launch F/A-18's and at full alert, launch F/A-18s every thirty seconds thereafter.

***

President Li knew the Chinese Rocket Force had successfully test-fired a missile that impacted and destroyed an orbiting satellite several years before. Additionally, he was aware the PLA later successfully tested and destroyed an incoming test ICBM with a modified DB-26 missile. President Li realized they had the technology to destroy a satellite in orbit and destroy a missile in guided trajectory. And yet, he mused, the Americans foolishly believe their carriers indefensible?

Since its deployment, the Chinese satellite had trained its optics on the American satellite—which was covering a forty-degree angle over the South China Sea. It had been patient, like a hunter waiting in a stand for its unsuspecting prey. The Chinese satellite had never taken any image of a weather system, nor was it ever intended to. The PLA ground station sent an electronic encrypted command to their waiting weapon in low orbit. Immediately the Chinese satellite sent quick impulse lasers at its programmed target that initially appeared to do little damage to ComSat5. The American satellite optics still worked. Its geo-positioning still worked. The data downlink, however, was now critically damaged and inoperable. It would take the Americans several days of satellite commands to realize their ComSat5 was nothing more than another piece of orbiting space junk. It would take even longer for them to know *how* it had been rendered useless.

***

As dawn rose over the South China Sea and the first light of day shone in the sky, a group of twelve Chengdu J-20 Dragons took to the skies from Spratly Island Base. The Chinese hunter satellite now came to life with new commands from the Chinese ground station. The satellite began searching for the signature program of a carrier strike group. The search did not take long. CSG-5 had been found less than 500 miles from the Chinese air base. The chairman gave the order: "Operation Dragon Storm is to begin." The terrain of Spratly Island is hills with low pockets. These were ideal hiding places for mobile short-range ICBMs that can strike from 300 to 3000 miles. More were concealed while building the artificial island for the PLA air base. Mobile launchers fired DF-21s and 26s in quick succession. Twelve short-range ICBMs were trained at the strike group carrier with their guidance systems accurately receiving satellite information. They launched simultaneously. Without the Comstar5 satellite optics, the first warnings came from the Hawkeye and the Global Hawk JSTARs to all commands in CSG-5. The group began tracking the incoming missiles as the Arleigh Burke destroyers began countermeasures. The Ticonderoga-class cruisers went to battle stations!

Col. Wei gave the order for his J-20s to engage the enemy strike group's carrier on his orders. The pilots began activating their missile radars and signatures targeting the American strike group. They were only minutes from launching their overwhelming barrage of *Qiangda* cruise missiles. These cruise missiles were as new as the aircraft. Formerly only Chinese bombers were equipped with much larger cruise missiles. The *Qiangda* cruise missiles were smaller yet faster and very accurate with satellite data. The carrier had advanced AN/SPS-48 air search radar which picked up the incoming fighters. The J-20s anti-radar feature minimized their signature, but they were not as invisible as they thought. Nor was the carrier the big slow target they expected. The carrier had already brought both A4 Westinghouse nuclear reactors to one hundred and five percent power! Four steam turbines drove the four large shafts of the carrier to an extreme speed, and both destroyers and cruisers struggled initially to keep formation protection.

China's advanced WS-15 engines, high speed and fuel efficient, were now a tactical advantage against the American fighters who were well within range. The destroyers prepared for their own missile launch despite many incoming threats detected as Aegis lit up the screen. The *USS Fitzpatrick* was the first to fire Sea

Sparrow surface-to-air missiles—followed quickly by other surface ships. Several incoming ICBMs were destroyed, but not all. The carrier's Phalanx system turned quickly to port and fired as the first wave of ICBMs closed in. Black smoke billowed into the air as the Phalanx fired rounds at a staggering rate of 4,000 rounds per minute against the lethal missile attack! Six missiles disintegrated just short of the carrier's port side. Two more missiles were quickly destroyed, and one hit the carrier just as another F/A-18 was launched.

As the Chinese, with over 12 J-20s, closed in at 200 feet above sea level, Col. Wei gave the order to attack. Each Dragon had two recessed wing-mounted cruise missiles and two air-to-air missiles in reserve for response against American fighters. For penetration, the fighter had four retracted long-range missiles (AAMs) with active electronic scan arrays (AESA). In rapid succession each plane successfully launched its wing-mounted *Qiangda* missiles. A second massive wave of missiles was only a few miles away and closing quickly!

The Dragons did not turn, they advanced confidently, with each plane holding secondary missiles. Every American strike force vessel had the ship's battle alarm blaring! Adrenalin-filled crew members responded with training and skill, remaining in battle position on full alert, weapons armed and firing as the J-20s approached. The destroyers closed slightly tighter to protect the carrier. Each destroyer was equipped with AN/SPY-1 phased radar systems. They knew the Chinese air attack was unfolding fast! A swarm of cruise missiles filled the radar screens. The Arleigh Burke destroyers locked on with surface-to-air missiles and fired. Cruisers fired anti-missile weapons. The Chinese cruise missiles were low and fast. As the deadly wave approached, another F/A-18 took off, with another being readied. A series of five guided missiles slammed the side of the carrier and the control tower as another cloud of black smoke billowed in the air! The combat-ready carrier hardly shuttered as she moved forward defiantly, circling to starboard with support vessels close by. The *Washington* fired heat-seeking missiles that radar tracked on the fast-moving Dragons. Three Dragons never saw the missiles hit them! Smoke trailed the carrier as the crew's anti-fire personnel worked feverishly.

Col. Wei gave his final order of Operation Dragon Storm. "Strike only the carrier!" There were too many Dragons moving too fast! Another swarm of Dragons launched missiles that hit the flight deck.

Fighters still on deck were caught in the blaze, and soon American ordnance exploded on the carrier! The Dragons came in low and now encountered several F/A-18s, which fired air-to-air missiles at the oncoming intruders. The skills of the American pilots were far superior to that of the Chinese. Using the F/A-18s highly effective front-mounted 20 mm M61 Vulcan cannons, several J-20s were splashed before they could fire their last missiles. The American pilots had yet another advantage over the Dragons—the F/A-18s counter measures and advanced electronics told the pilots in what order to kill the enemy targets. The Chinese had no such advanced system, and their pilots soon found their targets too late to maneuver. The remaining Chinese fighters communicated with Col. Wei. The carrier was stuck heavily but was still under power. Many J-20s were lost, but those still flying were ordered back to base. As the attack subsided, Col. Wei's communications were instantly sent to Beijing.

With quick assessment, the military planners in Beijing copied the North Korean Military Commander Kim Wang Un.

The confusion to the American command was deliberate and alarming!

The Pentagon, Washington, DC

As information came into Command and Control, the situation was dire. The US military went to defense condition 2. This fight by the Chinese was not entirely expected. CSG-5 with a nuclear Nimitz-class carrier was severely damaged, listing ten degrees to port, but still afloat and moving not to Japan but to Pearl Harbor—provided they could make the long journey without further engagements. Nearly two squadrons of Chinese J-20 Dragons were lost along with many pilots. It directly cost millions of Chinese yuan in lost aircraft and cruise missiles sacrificed for this conflict. Casualties were not yet assessed, but it was bad. The damage to the carrier, however, was *incalculable!*

***

The Chinese military knew they had given the Americans one hell of a fight. It cost them heavily as well. They did not, however, sink the carrier. Would the Americans unleash a wave of missiles from land-based installations? The Chinese military tacticians doubted an escalation as the American vessels were within their sovereign waters. They further believed correctly that no American president would consider nuclear options—particularly when the Americans were, in their view, the aggressors. Did the Americans have a new weapon? The Chinese bases remained on the highest state of alert over hours, then days and weeks. No counteroffensive came. President Li had masterminded the attack and caused confusion to preempt American counterattack. "Ia Chi," Col. Wie later said to his staff. "Attack a superior enemy from the sides and weaken him. We will go for a kill another day." Col. Wei knew that Dragon Storm included yet another element in President Li's master plan. President Li positioned an especially important ally prior to the attack on the American carrier… an alliance with a very unpredictable North Korea.

***

The Pentagon, Washington, DC
Six Months Later

The president addressed the joint chiefs, including Admiral Wilson of the Navy, Chuck Grimes of the USAF, Army General Collins, NASA officials, and newly assigned Dr. Adams, as well as new representatives from the US Department of Energy. In a strong and steady voice, he spoke, "A few months ago, one of our carriers was aggressively attacked by land-based missiles followed by air-launched cruise missiles from Chinese aircraft in the South China Sea. We lost some brave men and women, and one of our carriers was significantly damaged. This presents a clear and present danger to our carrier assets around the world and undermines our role on the world's geopolitical map. To be sure, we could have decimated the Chinese in a counteroffensive, but discretion and diplomacy outweighed further fighting... at least for now."

"I have with me today the National Defense Strategy Commission report that states we are losing our military advantages to China, Russia, and North Korea. North Korea is making long-range ICBMs with multiple nuclear warheads. Both China and Russia are moving steadily toward military dominance and claiming regions of the world—like the Arctic—where we have had little influence in the past. For heaven's sake, we paid the Russians heavily for transporting Americans to the space station for almost a decade." Only recently has the private sector developed new rockets with orbital capabilities. The president's voice grew louder, and his eyes narrowed. He projected outrage and incredulity.

"Both Russian and Chinese military leaders say their submarines, their air- and land-launched missiles, make our aircraft carriers indefensible in a protracted military conflict. Can we defend an aircraft carrier from enemy cruise missile attacks and simultaneous drone aircraft all from multiple directions? Can we stop new hyper missiles? How can we stop scores of missiles attacking a carrier like the Chinese did?"

"Our admirals still have confidence we can. They state in this report that our combat systems, weapon control systems, SeaRAM technologies, phased radar systems, radar-guided missiles, and other air search radar technologies can do the job. However, my report presently indicates we do not have the resources or military innovations necessary to take on either China or Russia in an ongoing conflict, short of nuclear options." The president paused as he again made eye contact with each man. His eyes shared unspoken words.

"I do not want us to wait for another attack to awaken from the complacency reflected in these documents. Ladies and gentlemen, you know I am more of a historian than a politician."

The president continued with deep-seated confidence. His voice was steady and strong. "We need a new platform with new weapon systems that will make missile attacks against us obsolete. A system that not only protects our carriers and surface vessels but protects Americans across the United States as well.

"From the dawn of the twentieth century, people like Lindberg and Earhart, the Wright Brothers, Eisenhower, Edison, Einstein, Carver and Archer, Murphy, Oppenheimer and Teller, Glenn and Armstrong…" As the president spoke slowly, he again made eye contact with individuals in the room. "These people all had spirit though they worked in different capacities, some civilian, others in different branches of service, they held various ranks, and attained various degrees of education. Their diversity exhibited the very fabric of this nation. When technology, ingenuity, and courage all come together, ordinary people become extraordinary!

"Space Operations was recently formed as an elite assemblage from all military branches of scientists and technologies. They will bring ingenuity to the forefront of homeland security and defense.

"Just as Big Safari's rapid implementation of existing and upcoming technologies led to extraordinary weapons for the United States Air Force, just as Skunk Works built incredible machines, and in the spirit of the Manhattan Project, today we support and fund Space Operations to make impossible weapons possible!

"Today, I announce Space Force Operations to be fully funded in order to utilize today's best technologies with tomorrow's undiscovered advances in space defense weapons and technologies."

The room erupted with enthusiastic applause! Everybody rose to their feet! A spirit of national pride swept through the crowd, and a feeling of empowerment settled quietly in the hearts of all present.

"They have been given extremely broad parameters and latitude… notwithstanding, Space Ops will report to the chairman of the Joint Chief of Staff and keep me informed as needed." The president spoke pointedly.

"This is a no-fail mission, ladies and gentlemen. Thank you for your support."

***

Shell Island off St David's, Bahamas

Moogo and Taren were cousins living in a quiet fishing village on a small island near the larger St. David's Island where tourists visited. The island was beautiful, and the beaches were pristine, but the bad economy kept the residents impoverished. Moogo, a seasoned fisherman at only twenty-three, had been fishing since he could walk, having learned the trade from his father. His young wife, Malini, was twenty-two. Together they were bringing up a son, Ramani, in a home rich with love but scant of more than basic food and clothing. On a good day, Moogo's catch may be nearly fifty pounds of fish, bringing eighty-five cents per pound at market. On other days, their small take from the sea was only enough for their supper. Malini and Moogo mended their nets as needed, and Malini supplemented their meager income by making straw hats from the vegetation that grew nearby. The small island airport was a perfect place to greet tourists and sell their crafts.

The little family worked together in the cool of the evenings to grow a small garden of bananas—always with an abundance to both sell and eat. For many years, their boat was a well-worn canoe with an outrigger on the side to prevent it from capsizing when sudden winds came up. They later bought a used twenty-two-foot fiberglass boat from an old friend. This boat had the added advantage of a ten-horsepower Johnson outboard motor made back in the 1960s. Though it was old, it could get them out farther than the canoe and into the better fishing grounds.

Space Operations
Washington

The Pentagon houses all branches of the military. Newly formed Space Operations has a duty to protect Americans with a growing mission in our final frontier. Throughout centuries, warriors have known that those who control the "high ground" have an advantage. That truth remains, but now the "high ground" is no longer a hill above the valley—it is space. The importance of space to our national defense is growing at a rapid pace. During the last fifty years, NASA has made great strides in space exploration; we have learned much, and yet we have only begun to scratch the surface of understanding that great expanse. During the 1960s, the air force, with assistance from brilliant engineers at Skunkworks, were responsible for many stunning achievements. Of note is the SR-71 Blackbird, which remains one of the fastest planes of all time and reaches altitudes over 115,000 feet. That was over sixty years ago. Where are we now in our quest to conquer the skies? Space still holds many unrevealed secrets.

Astrophysicists conclude we know a mere five percent of the secrets of the universe. We know stars, planets, and universes are expanding. This was discovered by Dr. Hubble shortly after the turn of the century. It was verified by Einstein. But, still, what is filling space as everything expands? Scientists believe space is not a void. Space can bend and ripple, just like a fluid. It is filled with something—a substance that was at play in the big bang that created stars, planets, and universes. Is the expanding space being filled with some type of invisible matter—"dark matter"? Was this energy from the high-speed collisions of subatomic particles? Dark energy is moving the universe. Its invisible mass reacts to the pull of gravity. It does not associate well with regular matter. We know particles can gain mass and force by going through certain fields. Many secrets remain veiled in mystery. A giant step forward to unlocking the secrets of the big bang was revealed through the particle accelerator.

In efforts to understand more about the secrets of space and new weapon technology, the Pentagon invested heavily in an eighteen-mile underground particle accelerator located in Maryland, outside the DC area. It was originally kept top secret, though it was difficult to hide the enormous costs. Scientists knew they were looking for the next level of particle weapon technology which they ultimately discovered—dark energy waves, enormously powerful but very power consuming.

Dr. Mike Adams arrived at the Maryland Space Ops. facility in his usual manner and took the elevator to descend five stories below ground. This was one of his first assignments and an operational merger from an early integration of Space Ops. There he met his assistant, Alice Wilson, at the control station where all lights were green—her "Christmas Tree" panel. Space Ops. had taken the former particle accelerator facility and slowly evolved it into our next platform for dark energy wave technology. Dark energy waves are different from basic particle wave operations and require an enormous amount of electrical power. The new facility was connected to the Washington, DC/Baltimore power grid with an additional hook-up to Virginia Dominion Energy to the south. Still, Dr. Adams was uneasy about the stress already on the existing power grids, additional power was not readily available. The risk of brownouts in Baltimore and the ensuing lack of power that would stop elevators, make subways motionless, and leave office buildings' climate unheated or cooled simply was not acceptable. Most of the country's power grids were expanded decades ago and not upgraded regularly due to costs.

The Basement

"The Basement" was a largely unknown and rarely visited area of Space Ops. Dr. Adams had a 400,000-gallon saltwater tank installed there, which was initially used to conduct experiments on tidal gravity—the impact of the moon and other orbiting bodies' influence on oceans and movement of great volumes of water. One of Dr. Adams' experiments was to understand how, exactly, gravitational waves affect the oceans and pull massive amounts of seawater with such seemingly relative ease. The experimental dark wave accelerator was built near DC specifically because of its close association with the Pentagon and the particle collider. Wallops Island was also a potential site, but as the program grew into space power technology closer proximity to power grids was needed.

The basement became a combination of laboratory and military platform, making it vital for all branches of the military. The president routinely met directly with top officials of the Navy, Marines, Air Force, NASA, Coast Guard, and Homeland Security to stay abreast of all phases of the especially important expansion of Space Ops. The president was eager for advances in technology that could revolutionize weaponry, security, and exploration as well as national defense. The newest recruits for Space Force were hand-picked from all branches involved and were noted as the best and the brightest. Quietly, NASA officials were also moving command of the International Space Station to Space Ops. Satellites formerly controlled by NASA and US Air Force were being turned over as well. Dr. Mike Adams was Space Ops. Director, but more important was his ability to interface the services for an even bigger experiment.

***

Dr. Gifford, Marine Biologist

Dr. Jeff Gifford was a lifelong marine biologist. He had made no new discoveries in marine biology but did secure ongoing employment with the navy, collecting data on the rise of sea levels and the warming seawater temperatures. The future of the navy was changing with global warming and the melting of polar regions, and Dr. Gifford had exceptional skills.

Jeff and Mike were old friends, although they did not see each other often. They grew up running together along the Outer Banks of North Carolina, chasing seagulls, examining shells, and a lot of surf fishing. During high school, they both worked as mates on fishing boats out of Oregon Inlet, becoming more and more attracted to the secrets of the sea, the power of the tides, and the wonders of forces at work between the

Moon and Earth. After high school, their careers took them in different directions. Jeff earned a degree in marine biology, eventually completing his doctoral degree with a thesis on the hidden effects of tides. Mike, meanwhile, joined the navy and rose in rank as he earned dual doctoral degrees in astrophysics and electrical engineering.

Despite the spin off to separate careers, Jeff and Mike remained close friends. They had a standing ritual of meeting for dinner on the rare occasions when Dr. Gifford had reason to be in DC. This time, Dr. Gifford was called to DC for a meeting with navy officials about the latest sea level trends. As usual, he called Mike to make plans for dinner at a popular steakhouse, The Butcher's Brother, not far from Dupont Circle. They met at the posh restaurant around eight p.m. and began chatting about high school football as the waitress brought them a round of drinks. After they reminisced about the fumbles and turnovers of their high school football team, the conversation turned to their families. Jeff lamented about the life of a marine biologist—poor pay and long sea departures, neither of which suited his ex-wife. Now, he was married to his career, and at least part of his life was simpler.

"I know the Navy is worried about their assets at Naval Station Norfolk and about what will happen to this low-lying naval base in twenty years, perhaps sooner." Jeff knew that he and Mike had similar concerns and a vested interest in the sea levels.

Mike sighed. "The ships and vessels aren't the problems, of course. It is the housing and other base structures. The bases are in a compromising position, and the Pentagon is weighing a cost-benefit analysis of potentially moving to a more suitable environment.

"Warming oceans are bringing more powerful hurricanes at an increased frequency."

"Naval Station Norfolk is the largest in the world, and heavy rain can make some low-lying areas impassable for personnel. It is the most at-risk base on the East Coast. They want sea level analysis for Naval Air Station Oceana, as well as geographically flood-prone bases in Florida and the Gulf Coasts. Some of these bases could lose fifty percent of their usable land in the not-too-distant future. Sea level rise is becoming an ever-increasing threat to many military installations and will come with a great cost not only to the military but also to the substantial financial concerns of the cities around them. When bases are forced to relocate, the local economy is devastated. Yes, the navy is extremely interested in my research."

"So," Jeff asked inquisitively, "did the wave accelerator unlock the mysteries of the universe?"

"Well," Mike responded, "I don't know about that, but we're moving forward with some interesting projects.

"Frankly, Space Ops. is still dependent on many departments coming together. It is pretty sad we had to ask the Russians to catch a ride to the International

Space Station for nearly ten years, isn't it? Now the private sector is providing rockets capable of taking astronauts to the Space Station as well. We have even secured financial backing from certain private sector people to send up more rockets with cargo to the ISS. You know, the Space Station is only 250 miles up, not that far—but very expensive to get to. And the age-old truth still stands—those who control the high ground have the tactical advantage. Remember America's response to Sputnik?

Jeff acknowledged, "Sure do. It really got us going in the space race."

Mike continued, "At the present time, we have made significant progress. When you combine dark wave technology with a space-based accelerator, you develop new things, immensely powerful new things." Mike finished his drink, and they both ordered rare steaks featured by the chef as the best steaks outside of Texas. "Jeff, I want you to come by and see me before you leave DC. I have something interesting to show you now that you have Space Ops. clearance."

"Fine," said Jeff. "I'm open Wednesday morning before my navy meeting at fourteen hundred hours. Does that work?"

"Sure."

***

Honolulu International Airport

Flight 262 was an overnight flight from warm Honolulu, Hawaii, to the much colder Chicago area. The older Boeing 727 was only partially full because most tourists returning to Chicago were not interested in boarding aircraft at one a.m. for the super-saver fares. As for Molly Crumples, a spunky, single, seventy-year-old frequent traveler to the Hawaiian Islands, she accepted the red-eye as what happens when you book at CAF.com. (Cheap Air Flights). Honolulu was Molly's haven where she could escape the Windy City to dream and relax—and it had the added benefit of giving her much appreciated relief from her arthritis, something she called her literal pain in the neck. These red-eye flights fit right in with Molly's budget and lifestyle, allowing her to make the trip time and time again.

***

Black Waves

Jeff Gifford arrived at the Space Operations Center and showed his ID to the guard on duty. A second security officer greeted Dr. Gifford and said he would escort him to the Ops. Control Room where Dr. Adams was expecting him. They entered an elevator and descended to a secure area where the guard handed Dr. Gifford eye goggles and ear protection. Alice was calibrating the instruments, and the high-velocity electric turbines were energizing like the sound of a jet engine revving before takeoff. Computer screens were lit across the room, and radio chatter bubbled all around.

Mike welcomed his old friend with a smile and a handshake. "Welcome to Space Ops., Jeff. I want to show you an experiment we did over five years ago. With your work on sea level rise, I thought you might find this interesting. First, let me introduce you to my team, the crackerjacks that operate the military's latest weapon system."

As they walked along, Mike identified the functions of the staff around them. "Electrical Engineering and Control EE-CON. Needed to increase dark high energy waves. Oversees the additional power grids now available, a crucial component recently added at the president's personal authorization. The grid includes Pennsylvania Power and Light, Tennessee Electric, and Kentucky Power.

"EE-CON Officer is Robert Kosinski, former Homeland Security." Kosinski was a lean, six-foot, forty-year-old loner. With no family or friends, he dedicated his time entirely to his work with Adams. "Here we have Accelerator Satellite Earth Interface, ASE, who calculates accelerator waves to satellite accelerator to target information. Refraction calculations. What atomic elements make up the target? Iron, steel, platinum, aluminum? Combinations?

Virtually any element can be targeted by our system, more on this later.

"ASE is Commander Laura Martinez, formerly NASA."

Martinez was a first-generation American whose parents had immigrated from Mexico ten years before she was born. At forty-one, she was still a pretty bombshell who had earned the respect of her peers through hard work and discipline. She kept her emotions in check but had a talent for bluntness without rankling feathers.

"Moving along, here we have Flight Dynamics Officer, FIDO, to calculate target speed, trajectory, flight path. To ensure commercial aircraft and civilian aircraft are away from test zones, Capt. Luke Secor, Army." Secor was the youngest of the crew at only twenty-eight. He was a whiz kid with aerodynamics whose mind was always engineering something—some way, somehow.

"Also assisting is Lt. Robert Henley, radar technician."

Henley, twenty-nine, was quiet by nature and had the ability to shut out distractions completely when focused on a task. While he was engaged with his work, he could store up every detail of conversation and activity around him, yet he remained totally attentive to work. A conundrum in action!

"Next is Space Telemetry Communicator, SATCOM, in control of satellite beam strength, size, and power. What size area is our target, and what power level to achieve results? SATCOM is Chuck Grimes, USAF and Big Safari Special Ops." Grimes was forty-four, and the second-oldest of the group. He was naturally talkative and friendly, always ready with a joke, and was known for pranks, but no one was more serious when on duty.

"Lastly, Communications and Tracking Officer, CATO, to communicate with airports, weather, and military assets. ISS as needed. Commander Jack Luna."

Luna was the oldest of the group, at forty-six. He was open and friendly, but a man of few words. He was artful with language, saying everything there was to say in only a few words. His facial expressions and body language gave away his easy manner and amicability.

Jeff looked on with respect at the assembled talent and experience. This team was top tier all the way!

"Five years ago, we didn't have the power to redirect sufficient numbers of black waves. We have our own diesel-electric power generators, but they are not adequate for what we need, so we tap into grids for more. Power grids at most cities are already old, poorly maintained, running near their peak capacity, and prone to failure. Substation transmission power can vary from 250,000 to 750,000 volts—that is where we tap in. Later in the grid are step-down transformers that convert power to 10,000 volts out to homes and businesses. The transformer by your house will step-down to 240 volts," explained Dr. Adams. "We need substation power to run this thing along with our generators. What are the two top reasons for power grid failure? Equilibrium in power and power drain. The project here at Space Ops. does both at the same time!"

"Alice, how is the reading on your console?"

"Systems ready, sir."

"Today, we will have two power grids, Dominion to the south and Baltimore/DC to the north. We will convert only four giga-tetron volts for today's experiment, although we can now go much higher—50 to 100 giga-tetron volts. Frankly we do not yet know how high is high.

"Newton knew the three key aspects are mass, energy, and acceleration. Einstein recognized gravity was, in fact, relative and moves in waves. This led us to our next step which involved black waves redirected by our recent space-based accelerator.

"Do you remember the media tried to get special access to Wallops Island for the first Eagle 9 test flights? It made all the big networks. The first flight was indeed a test, tried to land the boosters too. The rockets all flew fine, but the boosters took a while to figure out. Anyway, the second flight had our space station accelerator aboard, now one big unmanned station.

We tried to keep it away from the press and media by saying it was a NOA Weather satellite. The press kept saying it was a billion-dollar Star Wars weapon. They were off a little—the cost was way higher. It was the most expensive payload into space on a single rocket ever.

"Our scientists did not know what to call the new gizmo they created, so they called it the *Newton Project*. Let me show you the initial experiment. The physics are not only mind-boggling, but also immensely powerful and potentially dangerous."

"Okay, my interest is peaked! What's going on down here that's so secret?" asked Jeff.

"Okay, follow me," responded Mike as he showed Jeff around the giant 400,000-gallon pool.

Jeff moved closer to the water and joked, "You found a new fish? Let me guess, an electric eel!" Mike smiled.

Mike approached a nearby console and opened a small refrigerator. He took out a twelve-ounce can of Coca-Cola and moved next to Jeff by the tank. Mike opened the Coke and took a long drink. He smiled at Jeff, "You ain't seen nothin' yet!" He took one more drink, then put the can below the surface of the water until the can filled with seawater and sank to the bottom of the tank.

Jeff watched with interest and attention but made no comment. Lt. Henley was former USAF. He was the Space Ops. radar control technician for the Newton Project. He had the essential job of tracking transponders between the satellite to the ground whenever black energy waves were tested. Pilots of an aircraft accidentally flying through the focused waves could potentially lose control of the aircraft, and the results could be bad. It had not been tested.

"Alice, turn power up to four giga-tetron volts."

"Roger, four G-T volts, sir."

Status on the console?"

"Power level successful, grids holding. Christmas tree green."

"Lt. Henley?" asked Dr. Adams.

Lt. Henley responded, "Connection to satellite station accelerator confirmed. Refracting angles per calculations. No aircraft transponders next thirteen minutes."

"EE-COM?"

"Go."

"ASE?"

"Go."

"FIDO?"

"Go."

"SATCOM?"

"We are go."

"CATO?"

"All go, Dr. Adams."

Power increased as Dr. Adams went on to explain. "What we learned from particle collisions we took to another level, into dark energy waves, black waves. Actually, more like fast energy twisting waves we later found, reminded me of the double helix in a way. We knew it was rotating, and followed angular quantum mechanics. We aimed the high-speed kinetic waves at a refracting accelerator station in geo sync. I am now aiming the return waves back toward us! Do not worry, your body is sixty-five percent water, so you will not feel much effect, if anything, but in fact, you are being affected. Chemistry, you understand."

They all watched the tank of seawater. Slowly the water level began to rise at the end of the tank nearest them. They viewed the water level increase through the glass, and it measured almost 50 mm on the gauge.

"Notice the opposite end of the tank," Mike said. It was lower by 50 mm.

"You've created an indoor tidal phenomenon!" Jeff exclaimed in astonishment. He stared at the tank and saw something shiny near the top of the water. "The Coke can is floating! How can that be? Jeff, I made the most exciting breakthrough of my career, by harnessing the elusive 'Ghost Particle'. At first my observations were only for a few seconds. Even now, I can witness this for a scarce, few minutes, and that's only providing the power source holds steady."

Dr. Adams walked over to the console and removed a navy ship compass which was held in a wooden frame and pivoted on two axes. He showed it to Jeff. The needle was spinning very quickly as if it were motorized! "Imagine what happens to your navigation system if you rely on magnetic navigation, it's haywire!"

"I will explain it shortly. Alice, power down. Mr. Henley, disconnect satellite station link."

Immediately the Coke can sank, and the water level returned to normal. The compass stopped spinning and slowly came back to pointing magnetic north.

"Confirmed," said Lt. Henley.

"What I have shown you here today, Jeff, is a re-creation of *Newton Project's* first test. You did not really think the Pentagon was spending $18 billion on research for nothing, right? Newton's Law… 400 years later!"

Jeff remarked cautiously, "I've seen this with my own eyes. I just don't understand."

Mike removed his goggles and ear protectors and asked Jeff to join him in his office. They entered a small and humble office with computers, a bank of phones, a refrigerator, blackboards, and a noticeable quiet compared to the operations room. Mike went to the refrigerator. "A soda?"

Jeff smiled and said yes as he removed the goggles and protective ear covers. Jeff walked with Mike over to a wall that was covered with charts, graphs, and chalkboard calculations. "Well, it starts here, with the Periodic Table—a basic from chemistry class. Light elements to the left, starting with hydrogen, and ninety-two heavier elements, moving to the right with the heaviest, uranium. Atomic number above the element name and, more importantly, atomic mass below the name. And what makes the difference in their weight, or should I say their gravitational weight? The program you just saw was a calculation I made on the atomic mass of Al, aluminum, but it includes a spectrum that affected seawater, hydrogen, oxygen, as well as others, just as gravity affects all elements with mass or energy. All I have done is changed one form of energy to another, but with a difference this time. Black waves with enough energy to mitigate gravity.

"Ask most Americans if the sun is a burning ball, and most will say yes, which is totally wrong! There is no combustion taking place on the sun at all; it is fusion. It's lighter elements getting hit by heavier elements."

Jeff mused, "Are you telling me the sun is a giant particle collider?"

Mike continues, "While particles can transmit force, only very few particles are the building blocks of what we consider normal matter. The high-energy collider can create particles that gain mass, as they go through different fields, and therefore, different types of matter. Some particles we tested didn't react to the fields, whether magnetic, electrical, or gravitational, but we did discover some that reacted very strongly, such as particles with heavy mass that contained high-energy, which held it all together.

"Einstein knew light has no mass, but the space around it can be bent. Ask any astrophysicist what we know about the universe and gravity and they will have a similar figure, maybe five percent is all we know. Some thought gravity is transmitted by particles. Einstein called them graviton waves. When you can explain to me the Big Bang then maybe I can finally explain gravity.

"The universe is made up of stars, planets, rocks, gases, and we know it's expanding, so what fills in the space? Invisible matter? Dark matter? A strange recipe of subatomic particles? We think it's a type of dark matter in a twisting yet irregular pattern. Jeff, we are looking at what we know in a different way, looking past what we know for new answers, and open to investigating potentials."

***

Space Operations Meeting

Mike Adams arrived early carrying his computer and was surrounded by his staff of selected USAF, NASA, and now also official Space Force staff as his direct reports. In attendance were several of the Joint Chiefs as well as Grimes, USAF, who commanded the Big Safari strategic platform. Admiral Wilson of the navy and Commander Jackson and their staff were in attendance. They exchanged formalities and reviewed the latest back-channel reports on Russian and Chinese situations as well as the latest North Korean missile launches.

Adams addressed the staff. "Big Safari utilized successful components from different platforms and weapon systems into increasingly effective new weapons and technologies. This same innovative thinking has now reached new heights in bringing Space Operations our latest integration of systems. Phase one was understanding and unlocking the secrets of dark energy waves. We have known the waves existed from the big bang. There has been a dark energy, like a type of fluid, filling in space as the universe has expanded. We can track this as stars collide and create great energy. Fifteen years of work at the collider unlocked the secrets of quarks, also with an understanding of Ghost Particles. Why fifteen years? Why so long?

"First, we had limited funding. Our work has historically been deemed not that important. No one in the Pentagon has wanted to fund particle technology that might raise crashed planes from the seafloor. In 1945, the Navy lost five Avengers and fourteen men on one mission, yet Congress still cannot justify a cost to fund this research. The Manhattan Project was only allocated funding because Americans were desperately seeking an end to the war." Dr. Adams leaned back in his chair, but his eyes were bright with energy as he continued. "Jeff, what would you do if you could unlock a gravitational field?"

Mike looked at Jeff and whispered again, "What would you do?"

Jeff stared at Mike and said, "I honestly have no idea."

"We have recently received the funding, developed the various technologies, and assembled the specific talents to take us into phase two. More specifically, to direct black energy waves at ICBMs, soon cruise missiles, later submerged vehicles, crashed vehicles, perhaps sunken ships, and one day, hopefully, as detection for nuclear submarines. ICBMs travel 15,000 mph and higher—or Mach 20 more or less—but much slower from lift-off through acceleration. Our system uses the missile's acceleration phase before the missile reaches apogee and long before it begins its descent phase. We totally change the dynamics of its flight!"

***

Eielson AFB Alaska
Sixteen Weeks Later

Phase two began inside the icy Arctic circle at two a.m. in Alaska, nearly 100 miles north of Eielson Air Force Base. The missiles were in hardened, heavily protected hidden silos and miles from any road that a satellite could try to identify.

Dr. Adams was in his control center with his familiar team in the Basement. Located only fourteen miles from the Pentagon, he met General Westgrove as he entered the lower area of the Basement Control Room.

"Thank you for coming today, General. I have something to show you that I hope you will find extraordinary and the next step to our national defense."

General Westgrove shook his hand and introduced four members of his staff.

They greeted each other somewhat cautiously. The general quipped to Dr. Adams, "My team has already informed me that you operate a ten-billion-dollar fish tank here! Is that what we will see, Dr. Adams? Please tell me this is not the latest project that we funded."

Dr. Adams laughed but grew concerned quickly. His forehead wrinkled, and his face tightened with unexpected anxiety. Notwithstanding, Dr. Adams smiled and said confidently, "We are working on your next best defense weapon, and we are ready to show you how this works."

He was met by Admiral Wilson, who shook his hand with earnest. "Nice to finally meet you and see your team and control center! I have heard so many great things that you are doing with Space Ops., Dr. Adams.

General Westgrove was not only the highest-ranking officer in the armed forces, he was the direct advisor to the president, secretary of defense, and National Security Council. Dr. Adams knew if today's test failed, this would likely end his project and his dream.

Dr. Adams explained the test. "The missile intercept test today is twofold. Locate and lock separate missiles directed at different US cities, disrupt their trajectories to neutralize the threats.

"The ICBMs for today's test are under the control of Col. Whitman at Eielson and his staff. They will launch LGM-30 Minuteman missiles which were originally armed with 1.2 megaton warheads. These warheads have been replaced with dummies for today, but equal weight has been added per my request.

"As you recall, the first, second, and third stages of these missiles are Thiokol solid propellants, deemed unstoppable. These ICBMs travel at maximum velocity Mach 23, about 15,000 mph plus and have a set ceiling of 100 miles.

"In addition, these weapons utilize Rockwell inertial guidance systems, and during flight, this guidance is protected by Sylvania countermeasures. In short, gentlemen, once launched, these weapons are unstoppable and devastating in their destruction when nuclear tipped!

"Our experiment is to test two missiles simultaneously from Alaska to simulate a first strike from Russian launch sites. Our ICBMs, have been programmed to hit Washington, DC, and Norfolk, Virginia.

"If you have no questions, we will begin our test procedures."

Dr. Adams received notifications about the activities and verified his team was ready with their now-familiar cadence.

"EE-COM?"

"Go."

"ASE?"

"Go."

"FIDO?"

"Go."

"SATCOM?"

"Go."

"CATO?"

"All go, Dr. Adams."

Dr. Adams gave the order to launch missiles controlled from Eielson.

The ten-ton protective missile covers slid hydraulically away as the missile's engines were ignited.

The ground shook as the launch proceeded as planned.

The weapons gained speed quickly, with the solid propellant now activated.

Commander Adams verified control integration. "ECOM?"

"Power level green, 100 giga-tetron volts, grids holding."

"ASE?"

Martinez responded, "Locked on multiple targets. They are gaining altitude quickly, but we are confirmed, sir. Missiles subsonic."

"FIDO?"

"ICBMs are ascent, sir. Trajectories appear hot and right down middle! Gaining speed as predicted and right on course. About to go supersonic. Gaining speed and right on target."

"SATCOM?"

"Setting trajectory interruption. System applications good."

Adams quickly asked CATO for confirmations.

Martinez replied just as quickly. "We have both missiles. They are hypersonic. Targets at 240,000 feet, Mach 13.8."

"The Washington, DC, missile is locked."

"The Norfolk missile is also locked on radar and confirmed, but we have this missile with trajectory changing."

Minutes passed quickly as Col. Whitman asked for confirmation. "Do we need to self-destruct missiles, or does Space Ops. have them? Please reply."

"The ICBM targeted Washington, DC, was now Mach 14 and approaching 400,000 feet. Speed increasing. Missile projected to reach 100-mile altitude and travel away from Earth, actually skipping into space."

Col. Grimes reported, "Second missile heading for Norfolk is in guidance lock. We still have it but not with the power level intended… however, target now moving far out into the Atlantic Ocean!"

"My estimate is that it will splash about 1,000 miles east of Norfolk. The area is clear."

"CATO?"

"Missiles are benign, sir!" Admiral Wilson and Jackson stared at their screens in disbelief.

"My God," said Admiral Wilson, "it worked!"

"Two ICBMs could have been devastating. Instead, one is diverted into space and the second out into the mid-Atlantic."

There was spontaneous cheering and applause in the Space Ops. control room until Dr. Adams, beaming with satisfaction, quickly addressed the team. "What we have witnessed today is one of the greatest technologies of the twenty-first century, the Newton Project! With more time and development, and increased energy resources to drive this power," said Adams, "we can not only remove a deadly ICBM threat, we can return it to the country of origin!"

The room exploded into a cacophony of cheers and kudos. Admiral Wilson addressed Director Adams. "I see this platform not only for domestic defense but as additional protection for our carriers and other naval assets. If we were ever to lose a nuclear carrier in a present-day conflict, then the integrity of these warships would become suspect. That is not an option, as expressed by the president."

Director Adams reassured both the admiral and Jackson that the next test would include more than ten submarine-launched cruise missiles and scores of drone missiles from multiple directions. "Space Ops. only needs more consistent power to conduct the test, and this power source is being engineered at this time.

Within a year, Admiral, we think we can potentially integrate the system with the existing countermeasures."

Dr. Adams called his staff for a debriefing. As the group gathered around the meeting table, Dr. Adams was pulling data from their computers to better analyze the results. He spoke to his staff. "While today's experiment was partially successful, it is indeed only a next step. Our objective was to put both missiles into space... not one. While both missiles were taken off trajectory, a ten-missile attack would have overwhelmed us."

Laura Martinez spoke up next. "Sir, we had stable power during this test, but not enough to move two missiles simultaneously. We have to have more power for future tests, 200 GT-volts minimum."

Dr. Adams responded, "We have been working on this for years. We have more support now, but we need to figure out how to drive more conversion power from less electricity."

Robert Kosinski, EE-CON, added his comments to the review. "I think my refraction calculations were correct, but I agree with Martinez. We could not lock the second missile without more power. Today's experiment was primarily over land, so we did not lose additional power until the second missile moved over the Atlantic. As we stayed locked on the missile and the power was directed over the ocean, our energy went all the way to the ocean floor and was simply power draining. We encountered no ships; however, a large ship would not have even noticed anything unusual. We probably loosened up some metal trash from the ocean floor along the way, which still took some energy away from our missile focus."

Chuck Grimes from Communications SATCOM added, "We are still a long way from isolating collateral materials being picked up. We will continue to develop this; however, the military wants to see what we are capable of today. If we can save two cities from attack today, we can do more tomorrow. Our technology continues to improve."

"I think we have a bigger problem right now," commented Capt. Luke Secor, FIDO officer. "Junk on the ocean bottom and ships on the ocean surface are non-issues except nominal power drain. These missiles launched at two a.m. when there was little commercial aircraft to be concerned with. I doubt the Russians will launch a strike when it is convenient for us," explained Secor.

"We need to be able to isolate commercial aircraft from ICBMs before the military will endorse our system," expressed Jack Luna, CATO.

"Sure, they never saw a weapon system like we have developed, but we are far from operational as a new military defense system until we can separate aircraft and other objects independently."

"I agree with you, Jack," expressed Dr. Adams thoughtfully. "The Wright Brothers got a plane to fly when they didn't know if the engine should be on the front or the back."

"Maybe that's where we are with the Newton Project. Are we missing power potential with this machine? Do we have the engine in the right place?"

***

Hawaiian Flight 262

There were only forty-nine tourists boarding a plane that could hold 205 people. Like the cheap accommodations offered to these tourists, their flight to Chicago was a low-frills non-stop flight. The plane was a 727, incredibly old, but the aluminum fuselage still met FAA requirements, and Hawaii Island Airline was still flying them. The pilots, Capt. Grant and Co-pilot Murphy, were both seasoned pilots who had earned the heavily desired Hawaiian flight schedules.

***

Space Command Operations Room
Three Days Later

It was after eleven p.m. on a foggy, rainy night. A man approached the operations building entrance. Motion lights came on, and he was immediately confronted by the guard, Officer Sam Robbins.

Officer Robbins was initially startled and asked for the approaching man's ID as Robbins' right hand grasped around his 9mm Glock pistol.

"I'm Robert Kosinski," the man said confidently, "I'm with Dr. Adams' team."

Officer Robbins recognized Kosinski as a team member who had clearance and had been to the facilities many times.

He asked Kosinski why he was there so late and without Dr. Adams. Kosinski simply said, "Oh, Dr. Adams is on his way but had to make a stop. We have priority testing that can't wait—a new glitch we just found. We have a general visiting, tomorrow morning."

Officer Robbins allowed Kosinski access but stated firmly he was not aware of any tests planned for that evening and was not expecting visitors to the building.

Kosinski responded, "I can understand that, Dr. Adams wants to make a good impression on the general."

The room was unusually quiet, with only minimal equipment running.

Kosinski began flipping power switches to the energy accelerator and explained to Officer Robbins that a last-minute change had been necessary. "We've discovered a potential problem and must act to correct the situation."

Robbins directed him to halt all activities pending authorization from Dr. Adams. Robbins pulled out his secure iPhone and began a contact search for Dr. Adams.

Kosinski ignored the guard's instructions to halt as he moved quickly to turn on more equipment in sequence. Power grids, accelerator to satellite interface, radar systems, and CAPCOM, which controlled beam strength, size, and trajectory area. He entered new programming into the computer, including a change in atomic mass algorithms. The noise in the room became louder as he went through the power-up procedure.

The security guard approached Kosinski urgently and with an almost frantic tone in his voice, he told Kosinski he required authorization from Dr. Adams.

Kosinski feigned assent. He took a step away from the console and threw up his hands in a show of exasperation. "No problem. I will wait for you to get clearance, but you better make it quick. Dr. Adams directed me to get this done ASAP—it is critical!" With those words, he reached behind his back, pulling out a short barrel handgun. A red targeting beam went from the gun to the guard's forehead before the guard registered what was happening. Kosinski steadied his aim instantly and pulled the trigger twice in quick succession—once to the head and once to the heart. The guard went down and did not move.

***

Hawaii 262

Capt. Grant locked in the flight control data autopilot, which kept the plane at 35,000 feet. Most of his flights were typically quick island trips. By the time the plane got to cruising altitude, it was time to descend and prepare to land. The Chicago trip with the 727 was a recent addition to his schedule. The air was calm, the flight was smooth, and everyone was happy to be on their way to Chicago. Hopefully for the flight crew, the stopover in the Windy City would be brief and permit them a quick return to the warm Hawaiian beaches. The abundance of empty seats was unusual, but the airline was filling them on upcoming schedules. He welcomed the passengers to his flight and turned the cockpit over to Murphy.

Capt. Grant went for some coffee and struck up casual conversation with an attractive flight attendant. The conversation was all too brief as the flight attendant soon turned her smile to a different face, a frequent flyer she knew well. "Molly!" she exclaimed. "I thought you might be on this flight!" They exchanged quick hugs, and the attendant slipped Molly a Cherry Coke, her favorite. Molly reached into her purse and brought out some Hershey's Kisses, which the attendant quickly took with a smile.

Molly proclaimed, "I just love flying with you! I feel like I'm with family!"

***

Operations Room

Kosinski watched the satellite trajectory screen on the computer. Slowly, the orbiting satellite began to pitch to a new angle, programmed now to a new and unknown area. The Newton Project worked as intended, linking to the satellite and back toward its new coordinates. The dark waves reacted, and the power grid went from green to red on the 'Christmas tree', a problem. Any other time this would require a shutdown of the support system, yet Kosinski still increased the power to 150 giga-tetron volts. The sound in the room became deafening! With no one manning the other instruments, he was unaware of the commercial airliner. It seems Kosinski did not care; his motives outweighed any concern of collateral damage.

Hawaii Flight 262

Suddenly the plane bounced as if it had run into violent turbulence. Passengers screamed. Drinks spilled. Overhead storage compartments opened, and carefully stowed items flopped around the cabin. Capt. Grant lost his balance as he made his way back to the cockpit, grabbing a seatback just in time to avoid falling in the middle of the aisle. A series of warning sounds came as he entered the cockpit, and he clawed his way back into the captain's seat. "Murphy, what happened?"

"I don't know, Captain! We have pitch warning, and flight controls do not feel right. Maybe a hydraulic loss. Flaps are not responding. Auto pilot is now off."

Capt. Grant took the controls and pulled back on the attitude stick between his knees. The aircraft began to yaw left, then back right. The rudder controls seemed useless. The warning sounds continued. Capt. Grant knew he was moments from losing control of the aircraft. Capt. Grant went down a quick checklist in his mind. What could have caused this? He quickly ruled out his greatest fears: a bomb, fire, a mid-air contact. All no. The cabin was still pressurized as the oxygen masks had not deployed. He tried to bank left and then right, but the controls did not respond. He knew only one thing for sure, they were going to go down quickly. "Murphy, give me the altimeter reading."

"Roger, altimeter 45,500 feet."

"That's impossible! We must have an instrument failure. We were at 35,000 feet." Murphy noticed the familiar whine of the engines changing. He checked RPMs. "The RPMs are increasing! Suggest you throttle back, Captain."

"If we lose speed, we lose control." Capt. Grant had hoped never to speak his next words. He did not hesitate. "Mayday! Mayday! This is Hawaii 2-6-2 heavy. Do you copy?"

There was a slight delay from a startled controller. "Yes, we copy. This is Air Traffic Control. What's your emergency?"

"Lost flight controls, possibly hydraulics. Have no control of the aircraft, including instrument failure. What is our altitude?"

The air traffic controller looked at his radar screen and went silent. Grant repeated, with obvious urgency, "Repeat, what is our altitude?"

The air controller simply responded, "You appear…" He did not know what to say. He thought transponder failure, but that had never happened. He had never seen a commercial plane's transponder show an accelerating climb beyond believed ceiling capacity of a commercial aircraft. He called his supervisor. "Sir, we have Mayday. Hawaii 2-6-2 heavy."

Suddenly a group of air traffic controllers gathered around the screen with Hawaii 262. They were astounded at what they saw.

This was impossible! "Flight 2-6-2, what is your altimeter reading?"

Grant responded impatiently. "My instruments have failed! The aircraft altimeter is now reading the max of the gauge 99,999 feet."

The air outside the aircraft was quickly becoming thin and very cold. The engines coughed, shuttered, and went silent. The cabin lights blinked. Grant tried to restart the engines. What was happening? As the engines stopped running, the lights blinked again, and this time the passenger cabin lost power. Alarm turned to panic as the passengers continued to rock and bounce in the darkness.

Molly was still looking out her window and was amazed at what she saw. She knew they were not falling but could not explain it. She turned and shouted at other passengers. "Take a breath, everyone! Calm down and look out the windows! Look! Think about what you see! We are not falling!"

Soon, very soon, the shouting stopped as people struggled to look out the windows. The cabin became eerily quiet as the motion of the plane registered with the passengers. Slowly, passengers began to lean back in their seats, with mixed feelings of relief, disbelief, and confusion. Their hearts were pounding.

"Engine RPMs have stopped; we have no working instruments. Emergency lighting is on," said Murphy.

Capt. Grant looked out his window and stared in disbelief. The cloud cover below him was slowly becoming smaller. He had never seen such a thing. The adrenaline running through his body momentarily made the subsiding G-force unnoticeable. A stewardess opened the cabin door, hoping to find some answers. She looked at the pilots and said nothing.

"ATC Hawaii, this is 2-6-2. Do you copy?"

Grant got a hesitant reply.

"Are you OK?"

Operations Room

Kosinski was working furiously, and he programmed the systems quickly. His calculations had been worked and reworked many times before, but for his reasons only. Alarms soon began sounding that the power grid had been overloaded for too long and with too much power. He could smell the burning wires in the control room, and the computers failed quickly. The Christmas Tree of power readings were red, and systems were overloaded with massive failures that were threatening a complete loss of control. Dominion Power to the south went offline followed immediately by Maryland Power. An acrid burning smell enveloped the operations room. A fire started behind the computer consoles, and even more alarms sounded. Auto communications to fire departments were transmitted. An auto call included Dr. Adams. Kosinski fled the room and quickly went up the stairs and out of the building.

***

Flight 262

Capt. Grant felt a strange sense of forward momentum in the aircraft. As he unbuckled his seatbelt, he realized his hands were clammy. He rose on wobbly legs and moved to join the stewardess behind the cockpit to assess the situation in the passenger area. Murphy stayed in the cockpit, asking ATC for updates. Grant saw the oxygen masks dangling from the ceiling and knew their deployment was a sign of low oxygen levels in the cabin. Despite all the uncertainty of what might happen next, everyone seemed safe for the moment. Grant could recall no explanation from either his training or years of experience that defined the cause of this… this what? He barely knew what to even call the situation! As he bent to look out the small passenger windows, he saw darkness beginning to shroud the aircraft. He glanced at his watch, and even the time left him confused. He wondered if he were in shock. Grant returned to the cockpit and asked Murphy for air traffic control updates.

Murphy's face looked ashen as he reported back to Grant. "Captain, altitude is confirmed by ATC. They say we are at 500,000 feet and now losing altitude."

Grant looked out the window, and the image he saw was otherworldly, like an image from the early space days. He could see a hue emanating around Earth, hovering just above the curvature. He could have sworn he felt almost weightless. "Impossible," he muttered.

***

Operations Room

Adams ran through the hallways and took the stairs two at a time down to the operations room, where he joined emergency personnel. As he approached Adams, the fire captain showed his credentials.

Adams looked around in disbelief as he stammered, "What happened?"

The fire captain explained there was a fire apparently caused by electrical issues, which on a preliminary investigation, appeared to stem from a system overload. "More concerning," he said, "Security Guard Robbins is dead."

"What?" Adams reeled with the news.

"The death was not caused by the fire or any electrical problem. He was shot. This was certainly no accident."

As Adams tried to make sense of the situation, his cell phone sounded with an emergency call from air force warning radar personnel. They had been contacted by air traffic controllers following a commercial airliner experiencing an unusual anomaly. Hawaii 262 was caught in something not yet fully understood. What they did know was that 2-6-2 was at 500,000 feet. They were told forty-nine souls plus crew were on board, but they had no report yet as to the condition of the aircraft. As Adams was listening to this report, he heard another call beeping in from the emergency line. He immediately took the call. This call was regarding another bizarre situation involving simultaneous electrical failures at both Dominion Power and Baltimore/DC/Maryland Power. Dr. Adams was being blamed for both power failures on the grounds that his facility had exceeded the allowable power limits, in turn causing the enormous outages and affecting thousands of people and businesses. Such a massive power outage quickly became deadly serious as hospitals went to backup power, electric trains stopped, elevators became useless, and thousands of homes lost power.

Dr. Adams called an immediate meeting with his staff.

***

Hawaii 262

"2-6-2 to Air Traffic Control. Do you copy? Over."

"We are unable to follow you on our radar system. We are turning you over to Air Traffic Chicago."

ATC Honolulu could only convey to Chicago that 2-6-2 had a problem.

The first controller from Chicago responded as he tried to locate the transponder. "What is your condition?"

But it was not in the expected area of his radar screen. As the air traffic controller tried to assess the situation, he could not understand the information. This aircraft was so high it was almost off the screen. Must be supersonic, military, and have remarkably high ceiling capability.

"2-6-2 are you a military aircraft?" asked the controller.

"Negative," replied Grant.

"Captain, I think we have a transponder malfunction," responded ATC Chicago.

"2-6-2 what is your call sign?"

"ATC Chicago this is Hawaiian Air 2-6-2 heavy. We are a commercial Boeing 727 aircraft declaring an emergency!" said Grant more angrily.

Grant tried assessing his condition. "Aircraft is intact, engines out, cabin on electrical batteries, amount of breathable oxygen unknown. Altimeter stuck on gauges max 99,999 feet."

There was a pause as both tried to figure what the hell was going on.

"ATC, your true altitude is more than five times higher. That is according to our tracking data."

Grant, once again, was dumbfounded. "ATC, say again, altitude is…?"

"You are 500,000 feet and moving easterly. Are you air force, sir?"

ATC Chicago had several ATC members, and now management watching closely.

"We are Hawaiian 2-6-2 heavy. We have no engines, no instruments, cabin pressure unknown, altitude and speed unknown. We are Mayday. "The only air we have is in the cabin. It will not last long! I do not know what happened.

"Flight 2-6-2, we will get back with you."

The stewardess tapped the cockpit, and Murphy opened the door. Murphy stated the obvious. "I'm sure the passengers are panicked. What's the situation out there?"

Trying to look calmer than she felt, the stewardess spoke quietly, "The passengers were panicked for a moment, but Molly calmed them down! Can you believe it? Molly! I was announcing that we are not in immediate danger, but the passengers were growing more and more upset. As soon as Molly spoke, everyone got quiet. What kind of magic does she have? She handed out Hershey's Kisses to everyone, too. Now everyone is just looking out the windows. Molly seems to be enjoying this. I swear I'll make her an honorary stewardess if we survive this!"

"Just tell everyone to stay buckled in their seats."

***

Operations Room

Adams' team came together quickly. At first it seemed that everything in the electrical system was overloaded and that nothing in the control room was functional. Eventually, they realized that powerful surge protectors had saved some of their equipment. Backup batteries restored nearly all functions except the accelerator is not working.

Lt. Henley looked at the radar screen as it came back to life and identified an aircraft transponder. "Dr. Adams, we've had no reason to know what the Newton Project could do to a commercial airliner. I guess we will have to learn fast. We never imagined anything like this, much less simulated it."

***

Flight 262

Grant discussed their situation with Murphy. "Murphy, what we know for certain is that we gained altitude with unprecedented speed for an aircraft of this type. How this could possibly happen is quite a mystery to me. We need to assess our air supply and then see how in the world we can bring this bird down safely, if at all."

***

Col. Grimes greeted Adams. Adams succinctly put the situation as he understood it to Grimes. "It appears one of our staff came into the operations room, killed the guard, and energized the Newton Project without authority. The system overloaded, but before that happened, a commercial airliner flew into the target area."

Dr. Adams addressed his staff. "Ladies and gentlemen, the situation is grave. An airliner was caught in our system unwittingly and has only a limited supply of oxygen. A rescue may be all but impossible. Many homes are in an extensive brownout. The operations room is heavily burned and water damaged. Newton operating system is questionable."

Dr. Adams paused, then addressed CATO. "Laura, keep Hawaii 2-6-2 patched in over the speaker."

"Roger."

"Mr. Secor, how long to work a solution?"

"Hours at least to review an airliner, sir. Our work has been prioritized to test missiles."

"Mr. Secor, we have only minutes before we lose those passengers."

"I understand, sir."

"We must slowly descend the aircraft. Too fast, and the fuselage will not withstand the descent. To slow, and the aircraft will not have forward momentum to establish flight controls. Commander Martinez, can you double as our EE-CON?"

"Roger, sir."

With a trembling voice, Alice speaks up. "Dr. Adams, it appears Kosinski reprogrammed the system for something he was looking for, but I haven't figured out his algorithm. The atomic weights he programmed were 'wide', broad area focus, therefore lower power allocations per square area selected.

"He had no one to check transponders, and then 2-6-2 flew right into his personal experiment."

"Who knows what he was looking for, Commander. Kosinski might have been testing it for one of our adversaries… and at an extremely high price!"

"Okay, team, the longer we take down here, the less oxygen they have up there. Let's move!"

Col. Grimes joined the communication and spoke. "Capt. Grant, this is Col. Grimes with Space Ops. Do you hear me?"

"Yes," replied Grant. "Your transponder indicates you are a Boeing 727. Is that correct?"

"Affirmative," replied Grant.

"I believe production of 727's ended in the late 1980s."

"We still pass FAA, sir."

"Roger that, Grant. Is your 727 a 'B' or 'C' class?"

"I don't know," responded Capt. Grant with annoyance. "Is this really important? We are getting low on air up here. It's a 727, sir."

Co-pilot Murphy interrupted. "It's a 'B' class, sir."

"Why, Col. Grimes?" asked Murphy.

Grimes whispered to Adams, "I think I can buy them some time."

Then he addressed Murphy. "Do you have a toolbox in the floor panel behind the captain's seat?"

"Yes, I think so."

"Good. Go to the front fuselage side door and remove the floor plate with the screwdriver."

"Col. Grimes, that's the emergency ramp under there. Why in hell would I want to…" Murphy paused, then smiled cautiously. "I'm with you, Grimes." He was filled with new hope that was audible in his voice.

"Have you guys gone nuts?" asked Capt. Grant.

"Sit tight, Col. Grimes knows what he's doing!"

Co-pilot Murphy got right in front of Molly's first-class seat and removed a worn floor mat and the panel below it. Molly addressed Murphy. "The oxygen masks aren't working, and I don't know what has happened to us. But somehow, I know we are going to make it!"

Murphy looked at her and said with determination, "Damn right we are!"

Molly smiled serenely and took a sip from her soda.

Murphy went to the cabin and talked into the microphone. "Col. Grimes, the panel is off, and I can see the pressure tank to the emergency chute."

"Take the clamp to the black tube off the tank," said Grimes.

He loosened the long air tank attached to the emergency chute. He released the nozzle, and air began to fill the oxygen-depleted cabin. Pressure rose in the cabin with more breathable air. Molly looked at him and smiled.

Murphy returned to the cabin. "What's this about, Murphy?" asked Capt. Grant.

"As I recall, sir, the 727-C emergency chute was upgraded to carbon dioxide plus nitrogen to open the chute faster. But our aircraft, a 727-B, has a big tank of compressed air instead. I guess Grimes knows his aircraft."

Murphy picked up the microphone. "Col. Grimes, it worked!"

There was no reply, as Col. Grimes was busy.

***

Space Ops.

Col. Grimes was experienced in space telemetry, but this testing with so many lives at risk was different. He reviewed his data with Adams and Commander Martinez.

"If we wait to test the Newton Project programming by the book, they run out of air and die. If we are wrong on re-entry, they die. If they come in too fast, they die. If the power fails, they die. I'm not liking this, Martinez."

Jack Luna, CATO systems specialist, was next to speak up. He had grave concerns about the climate in the aircraft. "Dr. Adams," said Luna, "it's going to become very cold in that aircraft, sir. If that plane is in the mesosphere like we think it is, it is sixty degrees below zero. With no running engines, they have no heat. The fuel lines will freeze at forty below zero."

Dr. Adams looked at Luna and said, "Let's tackle our obstacles in order. If we cannot get the plane down in a controlled, gradual descent, then I guess the temperature does not matter."

Adams addressed his team methodically.

"The system failed at 150 GT volts, and to bring this plane down slowly, we need greater power for a longer time. If this fails, we lose the plane."

"What if we begin system engagement and reduce power until the plane reaches two hundred thousand feet, then re-engage to slow the aircraft for as long as power holds? We will not lose the grid. We hope we can 'support' the plane if it free falls."

Martinez agreed.

***

Flight 262

"Grant, this is Dr. Adams. Do you copy?"

"Yes, this is Capt. Grant, are we ready to try this?"

"Affirmative. All passengers and crew are in seatbelts and ready."

Dr. Adams went through his routine.

"Commander Martinez, ASE ready?"

"Go."

"Capt. Secor, FIDO ready?

"Yes, sir, we are go."

"Col. Grimes, SATCOM ready?"

"Roger that and go."

"Mr. Luna, CATO ready?"

"We're go."

"Christmas tree green," said Martinez. "Let's roll!"

The room came to life as the Newton Project's powerful electrical generators began to roar! The accelerator station was synced and began a slow turn in space, aiming its powerful system toward fast-moving Flight 262, now nearing the Southeast toward Florida.

"EE-COM status?"

"Fifty giga-titan volts and climbing! System polarization, satellite accelerator engaged!"

"FIDO?"

"Aircraft is in our control and commencing descent."

"SATCOM?"

Col. Grimes sighed as he reported, "Following initial descent, stand by."

Grant felt a small tug on his plane and then an empty feeling in his stomach, like a roller coaster free fall. He was definitely falling. The plane began a descent at thirty-three feet per second. Then the descent accelerated even more!

Martinez yelled out, "Negative polarization. We need to reduce power, or we risk potential total system loss. Christmas tree green now, but it can't hold long."

Adams gave the order, "Stop power."

Capt. Grant's voice came through clearly. "We're descending pretty fast, no flight controls until we get into denser air. Smooth so far. How do we look?"

Grimes' voice was calm and reassuring. "You're right on flight dynamics. We're going to pull you in nice and easy until you are able to retake control of your aircraft."

Molly took a sip from the soda the stewardess had just given her. She took a photo of the view from her window as the sunlight began to brighten.

An Apartment Near Dupont Circle in Washington, DC

Kosinski was watching the final quarter of the Steelers versus Cowboys. He watched a Hail Mary pass from the Steelers' thirty-yard line to the Cowboys' end zone. The quarterback sliced the air with a perfect spiral pass. Kosinski came to his feet with a Bud in his right hand and a left-handed fist pump.

Before his fist even came down, the FBI tossed a flash grenade through the window and simultaneously used explosive putty to breach the apartment door. Kosinski dropped his beer.

"Freeze!" ordered the FBI.

Kosinski pulled his Glock from his waist. As he raised his weapon, two shots rang out, but they were not from his Glock! Kosinski heard nothing more before he went down hard. He gazed upward as he was quickly handcuffed. Before Kosinski passed out, the FBI agent knelt beside him and whispered in his ear, "You have the right to remain silent... for the rest of your life!"

***

Flight 262

Flight 262 entered 250,000 feet and was accelerating while descending. Grant and Murphy still felt no push back on the controls, but they knew they would at any second. The rate of descent alarmed them just a bit, but their altimeter still read 99,999 feet, gauge max.

Grimes gave the order. "Slow the descent now. Martinez, power up to 100 GT volts."

"Roger that. Power is not responding, Christmas tree red and flickering. Situation abnormal."

The plane began a steep dive, producing several times normal gravity. This was far greater than the wings of the plane would be able to withstand when it hit thicker atmosphere.

"Maryland grid is coming online, and power is being restored, Col. Grimes!"

"Commander Martinez, power up and slow that flight down. They are in descent below 150,000 feet."

Capt. Grant felt the control stick and foot pedal push back against him.

"Murphy, start left engine." A low whine whirred as the engine slowly engaged. Suddenly, the cabin was awash in light. The altimeter and instrument panel lit up. Air slowly began blowing through the cabin.

"Starting right engine." Murphy adjusted the RPMs, and power was regained.

"Let's keep the nose down a little more and pick up some forward speed."

The altimeter slowed at 80,000 feet, and the plane nose pitched down fifteen degrees. After several hours of near weightlessness, the passengers were feeling the thrust of 2.5 Gs and being pushed heavily in their seats. Slowly, this lessened to 2 Gs. All the while, Space Ops. followed the plane on radar, satellite, telemetry, and communications. The smile on Grant's face soon flowed to his voice. "Falling below 50,000 feet and systems returning to normal."

"Air Traffic Control to 2-6-2. We still have you. Can you hold steady at 35,000?"

Murphy looked at Capt. Grant as systems on the plane returned to normal, gauges and instruments reset.

"Yes, we appear to be steady, and engines have restarted. Flaps and control surfaces feel normal."

"Hawaii 2-6-2, your nearest runway is Bermuda, but Miami International is also standing by for your emergency landing. Miami may be better equipped to help you if your landing is rough. You have your choice of runways."

The next communication was Grant copying back to Space Ops. "Thank you, Space Ops. That was a nice re-entry! ATC has us again, and we are in control at this time."

The Space Ops. team whooped with high-fives and back slaps. A successful operation! Disaster averted! Alice and Martinez were nearly overcome with emotion as they each gave Mike Adams a big hug. A relieved Col. Grimes looked at Adams, winked, and smiled.

Grant motioned to Murphy as he picked up the mic. "Thank you, Air Traffic Control Miami. We are not making an emergency landing. We will head to Bermuda. Thank you."

"You know, Murphy, I'm going to have a couple of mai tais when we get to Bermuda," Grant said with a smile. "Do you think anyone will believe me when I tell our story? We will be the first Hawaiian Air to land in Bermuda! What a hoot! That should get the press asking questions." They both laughed heartily.

The stewardess knocked on the cockpit door and addressed them with a broad smile. "How are you guys doing?"

They smiled back and said, "Just fine! How are the passengers?"

"They all send a message to you. 'Great job!' And true to form, Molly wants to know how many air miles she gets on this trip!" They all laughed even harder!

A Small Island East of St. David's, Bermuda

Moogo pulled his battered outrigger up on the crystal sand of his humble village. It had been another long day on the water catching fish. He might have sixty pounds today, maybe fifty dollars. Not bad. Young Ramani ran on the beach to greet his father, like he had done since he could barely walk.

"How was the fishing?" young Ramani asked excitedly. Moogo lifted Ramani and gave him the usual kiss.

"Fishing was particularly good today, Ramani! Like we could just scoop them off the surface! Mama will not believe what I caught!"

Malani was in the cabin preparing her island vegetables to cook with today's fish. Moogo divided his fish, with some in a basket to take to the village market and some left in his old fish pail to take home. When he reached home, he set the pail on the table, next to the evening candles. Ramani peaked into the pail. "Bring me a good fish," his Mama said as she did every evening.

Ramani lifted a nice fish from the old pail and stared down and was astonished at the light flickering against dozens of incredibly old gold coins…

www.ingramcontent.com/pod-product-compliance
Lightning Source LLC
LaVergne TN
LVHW091601060526
838200LV00036B/947